Margaret MacPherson

THE BATTLE OF
THE BRAES

COLLINS
ST JAMES'S PLACE
LONDON

ISBN 0 00 184060 6
© Margaret MacPherson 1972
First published 1972
Printed in Great Britain
Collins Clear-Type Press
London and Glasgow

Contents

1 *Black Murdo*

It was a fine day for the time of year, and that was why we had wandered so far up Ben Lee. The wind was from the south-east, as it often is in autumn, and a haze with it so that though we were high up on the shoulder of the hill as it bends backward from the sea we could see little or nothing of the hills to the north of us. The grass had turned reddish brown on the moors which rolled away in folds at our feet.

Now I am in a wee bit of a difficulty here. You see in Skye we are Gaelic speaking and we are named differently from people in the south. We do not use surnames but are called after our father's first name. For instance, I am Somhairle Aonghais which means Samuel, son of Angus, but that is too much of a mouthful for the English and the spelling is difficult so I shall just call myself Sam. My surname is Nicolson but then nearly everyone in Braes has that for a second name except Archie, the boy who was with me that day. He is Archie Neil Ceannaiche—Archie, the son of Neil, the merchant and his surname is MacPherson.

Well, Archie was striding along ahead of me. I used to think he was everything I would like to be, tall and thin with a lean sharp face, pale in winter and brown in summer but never freckled. Now you will guess from that what I am like myself, round faced and freckled and, worst of all, with a thatch of red hair. It is a great misfortune to be red-headed and many's a time I was envying Archie his black hair.

But there was one thing I did not need to envy him—his bitch, for I had Ben. Ben was a big, deep chested, black and tan sheep dog. He was young, not grown to his full strength but already I could not tire him. I was busy training him and I looked round now to make sure he was at heel. It's the first lesson you teach them. Yes, there he was and when he saw me looking at him, he wagged his tail as if to say —what about some work?

Coming over a rise we startled a flock of sheep. 'Way wide!' I shouted on the spur of the moment and he was off in a flash and round them and bringing them back in the blink of an eye.

'What do you think of that!' I shouted to Archie. He had seen it but all he did was to shake his head.

'My Floss could do that before she was a year!'

'Oh! aye, going round hens, no doubt! Ben's not much over the year and he's getting better every week! There'll not be the like of him in Braes from end to end!'

But Archie just stood there, whistling low between his teeth and that provoked me.

'I'll show you then! You'll see for yourself. I'll put him on guard over these sheep and you and me'll go out of sight and I wager he'll stay keeping them together till we come back!'

Archie shook his head and gave a snicker of a laugh. 'Never come day,' was all he said. He could be annoying at times and this was one of them.

Now I had only just begun to teach Ben to stay on guard but we hadn't done it very often. Well, how could we with only ten sheep of our own and Ian after me all the time to leave them alone? But anyway, I'd have to try now so I went up to Ben and ordered him to clap, meaning to lie down. He wasn't too keen, but he did it at length, watching me all the time. 'Sit now!' I said. 'Sit there and don't move.' He lay there as good as gold, his eyes on my face. 'Now you'll see something.' I boasted to Archie. He grinned. 'I'll see something sure enough.' Off we went but hadn't covered twenty yards when I could hear Ben panting after me. I gave him a telling off and he dropped his ears and his tail and slunk to heel. Archie was having a quiet laugh to himself.

'Just you wait! I'll make him do it yet.' So back down I went. The sheep had all scattered of course and first we had to round them up. Then I made Ben lie down and told him to stay there. He lay down with his head on his paws, an anxious look in his eyes. I climbed back to Archie and we went on. At the top of the rise I looked back and he was in the same place, a picture of obedience.

We went down the slope till we were out of sight and then sat down. As the minutes passed and he did not come I began to feel proud and was just saying, 'I told you he'd stay!' when he came bounding on top of me, his tongue out, licking my face. Archie threw back his head and went off into one of his silent laughs till you'd think if you didn't know him that he had a bone in his throat.

'You rascal!' I cried and made to throw a stone at the dog so that he leaped away.

'Och! let him be, Sam,' said Archie when he could speak. 'It takes a time to teach them that one. They don't learn that in a minute. They hate being left behind.'

Well, that was true enough and come to think of it I had all the time in the world to teach him it. We strolled on crossing a deep gully full of rough stones and came to rest under a line of rocks. Archie picked blades of grass and putting one between his two thumbs tried to make a loud whistle.

I sat there thinking about sheep and about how once the whole hill had been ours.

'Archie! Do you think we'll really get the hill back next summer?'

Archie went on with his whistling for a little but then throwing away the grass he twined his long arms round his knees and considered my question.

'That's what they're all saying, your grandfather and my father and—och! everybody. It was promised to them.'

'Who promised it?' I asked. I heard plenty of talk though not much at home because of my Uncle Donald but I never could get anyone to go right back to the beginnings of things. They seemed to think I should know it all by instinct.

'It was the factor to Lord Macdonald promised it. Corrie they called him. He was good at making hard bargains. He took the hill away from the Braes crofters and gave it all to one man but he promised when the lease ran out that they'd get it back.'

'And the lease runs out next year?'

'That's right. It was for seventeen years. Corrie took it away before we were born.'

'We were nearly born!' I objected because I like to be in on things but Archie is a stickler for accuracy, a thing I never had much liking for and he shook his head.

'No, that was in eighteen sixty-five, over sixteen years ago and I'm just fourteen and you're not fourteen yet.'

I sat thinking for a while fondling the top of Ben's head to show I had forgiven him for letting me down.

'It must have been grand to have a lot of sheep!'

Archie nodded. 'Yes, wool for blankets and clothes and meat sometimes, braxy anyway. Even if we get the hill back this summer we haven't stock to put on it.'

But this was too gloomy for me. 'It won't take long working up a stock! We've all got a few and the ewes will have lambs and then the lambs will have lambs and—'

'Good life! They don't have lambs as quickly as all that, Sam.'

I chuckled. 'I know they don't but we'll work up a good stock in time.' And I sat there picturing myself and Ben with a huge flock in front of us slowly coming down the hill at shearing time.

'There's one thing we'll need for sure and that's good dogs!'

'Huh! I was hearing Ben was that good he knew it all already!'

'He's good right enough, Archie, but he needs practice and that's all. Come on! We'll round up a few more sheep before we go home.'

But Archie shook his head.

'Better not, Sam, we've been making enough noise as it is. For all we know Black Murdo may be over the next rise. He's the one to be out on the hill every day and with this haze we'd never see him. Look! we were seeing Loch Fada when we sat down and now it's gone.'

I looked down where he pointed and sure enough the loch lying at no great distance below us had disappeared from sight.

'Well! if we can't see he can't either,' I retorted, rather pleased with this argument, but Archie didn't think much of it.

'We'd hear if there was anyone about!' I went on, thinking him a bit of an old wife. 'Listen!'

Not a sound came to us but the sough of the wind in the grass and the far whistle of a curlew.

'We'd hear Murdo shouting to his dogs miles off!' I said. 'Oh! come on, Archie. The grouse would warn us long before Murdo could get near. Don't be so scared! See! I'm going to send Ben down below and make him bring in all the sheep he finds.'

'He'll leave the half!' mocked Archie and I was glad he was throwing off his caution. I wasted no more time in words but sprang up and ordered Ben to go 'way wide'. He was off in a flash but at the edge of the slope he looked back—I can see him yet!—ears cocked, one paw in the air, every line of him saying, what next?

I ran a few steps waving my stick and crying 'Way off, man! Fetch them, lad.'

He understood perfectly, gave one short, sharp bark and made off. Floss whined and shivered at Archie's side longing to join in. Archie was standing, a doubting look on his lean face. Just you wait, just you wait, I muttered to myself as the minutes crawled past. I kept shifting from foot to foot as if I was standing on nettles but just as I was giving up hope I saw the first sheep streaming up from below. I fairly sprang into the air with delight I was that pleased.

'Look at that! Look at that! You said he wouldn't and—' I never got the next words out.

'Sam!' was all Archie said but at the tone I spun round and there, not twenty yards from us stood Black Murdo, his two dogs at his heels and his dark face blacker than I'd ever seen it with the rage he was in.

'I've got you now! I've got you now!' He could hardly get the words out, 'Got you red-handed! Worrying my sheep! You'll suffer for it, you wait and see. I'll see you're punished for it!' We stood dumb, gawping at him. He was a tall, broad shouldered man, with black bristling eyebrows and a black beard. Everything about him was big, his nose jutting out and his hands grasping his long shepherd's crook.

'You thought you could do as you pleased, eh? Away up here on the hill and no one to see you, was that it? But I look after my sheep! I don't sit at home with my feet to the fire like the Braes men! I heard you all right and I'll get the factor on to you, that's what I'll do. He'll know what to do with the likes of you! Dirt! That's what you are. Dirt! There's a law in this country and you can't worry my sheep.'

At this I found my tongue. 'We weren't worrying them! I wouldn't worry sheep! I was gathering them!'

He thought I was being impudent—but I hadn't meant to be—and he ran at me, his stick raised. My feet acted for me and I dodged. He was like a bull charging, head down. He wheeled, charged again and again I side-stepped. If I kept my head and my footing he'd never catch me! I'd played this game many a time with my school fellows and I was champion at it. Black Murdo was too heavy and time and again his stick came down on the spot where I'd been just a second before. I was almost enjoying myself when, over the racket Murdo was making, I heard Archie shout 'Run for it, Sam, run for it.'

Yes! Yes! Of course, but the trouble was I had that line of rock at my back. He'd get me if I tried going up. I would not be able to climb quickly enough. Sweat was running down my face. I saw I'd need to dodge him a turn or two yet till I was clear of the rocks and had the moor to run over.

He was coming for me once more, lips drawn back, his yellow teeth showing, grunting from heat and fury. I sprang to the left away from the cliff. I danced on my toes pretending I'd jump to the right next time.

All at once his expression changed. He flung his stick, not at me, but past me. A dog yelped. Murdo went by me in a headlong rush. I went after him but too late. I saw Murdo's boot catch Ben in the ribs, once, twice. The dog howled in agony. Murdo swung round, grinning at me. 'I've finished *him*—now I'll finish you!'

I charged head down and caught him right in the stomach. He let out a gasp and heeled over flat on the ground. I stood there, staring, unable to believe my own eyes. One minute he'd been roaring and bellowing you could have heard him a mile off and now he was quiet as a stone.

Archie made to go near him but the two dogs crouched between us and their master, growling and showing their fangs. Archie tried to speak them fair but it was no use. They would not let him approach.

'He's breathing,' was all Archie could whisper, himself as white as a snowdrift. Could you call it breathing? He was making queer noises.

'He's just winded—that's what it is—we'd—we'd better be off, Sam, before—'

And that was a true word. 'Come on!' I said and now in a fever to be off I ran to Ben and grabbed him anyhow and he sank his teeth into my hand. At any other time I would have dropped him with the pain of it, but the fear I was in and the excitement lifted me up and I held on, telling him, 'It's all right, Ben. It's me. I'll look after you.'

We made off dashing down the steep gully, not minding the loose stones slipping below our feet, then out and down the long, heatherclad slopes. The weight of the dog dragged me down and the heather caught at my legs making me stumble but I did not fall. Next we were on to a patch where the heather had been burnt in the spring and the sharp, jagged ends cut the soles of our feet, hard as leather though they were.

The faster we ran the more terror stricken we grew but at last when we reached the turf dyke I knew I was done. I could not go another step supposing Black Murdo had his hand out to grab me. I just managed to put Ben down gently and then I lay panting like a smith's bellows, my breath rasping in my throat and a sort of redness before my eyes.

After a long time I pushed myself up and scanned the hill. Nothing moved, neither man, nor bird, nor beast. 'The brute! the dirty brute! to hurt the dog!'

'Aye!' said Archie.

I was in a sweat and yet the funny thing was I was shivering too and my teeth clattering.

'I was too slow, I was too slow!' I groaned.

'You did grand!' Archie exclaimed to my surprise for he was never very free with his praise, 'I never saw anyone that size knocked down so neatly—and you so small!'

I could have done without that last bit.

The early winter evening was closing in.

'I was too slow, too slow!' I kept muttering. My own stupidity was stinging me inside and I had to come out with it.

'Well, so you were,' Archie agreed and I felt like hitting him. 'What kept you dancing there when you could have made a dash for it?'

'I don't know—well, I had to keep my eye on him and then—ah! I don't know. Come on. It'll be dark soon.'

'Shall I take the dog?' Archie asked. I nodded, the fact being that now I was afraid to go near him in case he bit me again. The blood had caked on my hand but the wound smarted. As I watched Archie I had time to wonder how I could act so brave one moment and be such a coward the next. But Archie managed better than I had for he talked quietly to Ben first and then when he picked him up the poor brute whimpered but did not bite.

We walked slowly the last half mile. Now we could see the houses down below us and the blue smoke of the evening fires rising up from the thatched roofs.

There was a gate in the dyke behind my home but if we went that way we would have to pass Effie Uisdein's house first and she was a gossip and a mischief maker so we kept along the side of the dyke till we came to the other gate and then walked back.

My mother was hanging the three legged pot on the hook above the fire.

'Is that you, Sam?' she called cheerfully. 'I was wondering what was keeping you.'

'It's Ben,' I said, 'Ben—he's been hurt.'

'Oh! good life, what happened? Here! put him here, Archie. Oh! poor Ben.' She made room in a corner and Archie put the dog down as carefully as he could.

'Is he hurt bad, Sam?' Mother asked looking puzzled. 'Did he go over a cliff?'

'No, no, it was Black Murdo! He did it. He hurt Ben. He meant to.'

'Black Murdo!' my mother said, astonished, and at that moment my brother Ian came in.

'What's this? What have you been up to, Sam?' he asked but just joking. It was a different matter when he understood what had happened. He got a grip of me by the shoulders and shook me.

'You're out of your mind, boy! You let Black Murdo catch

you chasing Mackay's sheep! We'll get turned out for this if the factor hears about it. Out at Whitsunday, all for your folly!'

Mother sat down as if strength had gone out of her.

'Oh, Sam,' was all she said, but it hit me worse than Ian's hard words.

'We didn't see him!' I protested. 'There wasn't a sight or sound of him and I have to give Ben practice because when we get the hill—'

But this made Ian angrier than ever. 'Can you not tell the difference between taking the hill back which was ours anyway and chasing another man's sheep? Are you a half-wit or what's the matter with you?'

I should have had the sense to stay quiet and let the storm blow past but my tongue is too ready.

'We weren't chasing them! We were just gathering them. The ewes are strong at this time of year and it doesn't do them any harm!'

'You tell that to Murdo!' Ian growled. That was just what I had done but Archie gave me a dig in the ribs with his sharp elbow and I shut my mouth.

Ian knelt down and ran his hand gently over the dog. When he got to his feet he gave me a cold look and said, 'You act the fool and it's the dog that suffers.'

His words went through me like a knife and I felt miserable. If only I could have the day all over again I would act wisely and never go near Murdo's sheep.

'Will he get better, Ian?' I asked.

'He's got a broken leg, but that's nothing, it would mend but I doubt there's worse than that.'

'Grandfather will cure him!' I exclaimed, 'Oh! I know he will.'

My father had been drowned when I was small and my grandfather, Alasdair Bàn they called him because he had been fair haired, took my father's place. He was a slight, thin, wiry man with bright blue eyes in a thin bony face.

He came up to see the dog and I took it very much to heart when he blamed me just as Ian had done.

'Your mother has troubles enough without you adding to them, Sam.'

'Black Murdo has no right to kick my dog!' I muttered sulkily.

'Maybe not but you've no business moving his sheep!'

'They're on our hill!' I was sure I had him there.

'Aye! so they are but still they're Mackay's sheep—' He was busy examining the dog as he spoke and left the sentence unfinished. He set the broken leg but shook his head. There was something else wrong, he said, as he took out his pipe and tobacco, but he had done all he could.

'Will he—will he—get better, grandfather?'

'I don't know, Sam, I don't know, but if he's going to die he'll get out of here. They like to die alone.'

I felt so bad I had to go out. It was knowing I'd got Ben hurt through my own folly. I could hear Archie telling me not to send the dog after the sheep. I'd thought him soft and I hadn't listened. I stood out there in the darkness wishing I had.

2 *The Deputation*

I woke next morning with the feeling that something was badly wrong but what it was I didn't at once remember. And then it all came back and I was out of bed in a bound and through to the kitchen, my grandfather's words running in my mind, 'If he's going to die he'll get outside!'

But he was there, safely in the corner, and better still, when I knelt beside him and stroked his broad head he put out his tongue to lick my face.

'Oh! Ben, lad,' I whispered, 'You're better! You're not going to die, not you! and we'll be out after the sheep together yet, old boy.' And he wagged his tail and whined as if he understood every word I was saying and I'm sure he did.

Freed from my anxiety about Ben I had time to notice what was going on. Ian was all dressed up in his best clothes and Mother was brushing his jacket while he kept telling her it was good enough, it would do that he must be off or the others would be away without him.

'Where are you going?' I asked. It wasn't time for the Martinmas Fair and no one had died that I knew of so he couldn't be dressed for a funeral.

'Och! Mother, that will do,' he said ignoring me. 'You'd think I was a horse you were getting ready for market!'

'Oh! aye, or a man getting ready for his wedding.'

A flame sprang up from the peats and by its light I could see that Ian had got red. Why would he get red for a thing like that?

'A deputation's maybe as bad as a wedding,' he said with a kind of laugh.

'A deputation? What's that?'

'Oh! you be quiet,' he answered angrily, 'Any chance we had you spoilt yesterday with your tomfoolery!'

'Any chance of what?' I persisted. Well! I wanted to know. Ian looked as if he wanted to clout me, but Mother cut in.

'Father did say your best chance was to go at once before Alasdair Ruadh hears about the sheep.'

'And who's to know he hasn't heard already? Wouldn't Black Murdo go at once to John Mackay and John Mackay'd go hot foot to the factor!'

Ian was busy brushing his hair while he spoke and I was glad it was his own head he was using the brush on and not me.

John Mackay was the butcher who rented Ben Lee from Lord Macdonald. Black Murdo was his shepherd, though to hear him talk you'd think he owned every sheep on the hill, but he didn't own one. The factor's real name—I mean his English name—was Macdonald. He got the name Alasdair Ruadh because he was red-headed and I wondered did he mind being red as much as I did.

Mother gave a big sigh and said she'd imagine he would. 'But your grandfather knows him and he says Mackay is always putting off doing things but—' and here she broke off because Uncle Donald had opened the door.

'Oh! is it yourself, Donald?' she said and she hurried to fill a bowl with porridge and to put it in front of him.

Uncle Donald had come to live with us to help Mother when my father was drowned. But Ian was big now and Uncle Donald had become a catechist and was often away. He sat down, folded his hands and said a long grace. He had straight, straw coloured hair and his face was pale and straight too. He wasn't much older than Ian but I always thought of him as old for he was so quiet. If he spoke at all he weighed every word and out of doors he walked with a slow step.

I could see that Ian was itching to be off and the minute the grace was over he took leave of us saying to Mother, 'I won't forget your needles and thread.'

'Get me something!' I cried and then wished I hadn't for Uncle Donald looked reprovingly at me. Mother had dished porridge for me too so I sat down and began eating as quickly as I could but it was hot. I sloshed more milk on.

'Why did you not keep Ian from going on this foolish errand?' my uncle said, gazing severely at Mother.

Mother did not know what to say. She shook her head. 'He listens to Father, Donald, not to me.'

Uncle Donald pursed his lips as if he could have said a great deal but he wasn't going to. That was a pity because I might have made out what a deputation was. I'd have to hurry and follow Ian. I scooped up the last dribbles of milk, seized a bannock and made for the door. I could hear Uncle Donald telling me to wait for grace but not me! I was eaten up with curiosity.

We lived in the township of Gedintailor in the Braes. Our house was the highest, with the moors and Ben Lee behind us. The land goes up from the seashore like a stair with crofts on the 'steps' and rocks and bushes on each steep rise. Archie's house was directly below ours and Ewen Nicolson's was on the bottom step with the road running through his croft.

From where I was now I could see the Sound of Raasay running away to the north. The Island of Raasay lies opposite Braes and shelters us from the east but to the north there is no shelter. My grandfather used to tell me that there was no land between us and the North Pole and when the north wind blew, dashing huge waves against the rocky shore and the cold cut through me like a knife I could well believe him.

But the wind was from the south east and it was still hazy like the day before.

I could see Ian now striding away ahead going down the steep brae to the schoolhouse. At that I slowed my pace; indeed I was in no state to walk, my feet being red and sore from the flight through the heather. I kept on the grass and winced when I hit a small stone.

When I gained the top of the brae I saw a whole lot of people at the schoolhouse gate, boys as well as men and at that I tried to go faster for I supposed the boys might be going on the deputation too and if that was so I wasn't going to be left out.

There were six young men and I noticed that my Uncle Calum was one of them. I hardly recognised him, he was so spruced up. He usually wore patched trousers and a huge blue jersey with a large hole in it. Sometimes the hole was to the back and sometimes to the front. Calum was not particular.

'How's Ben?' Archie whispered.

'Fine!' I told him. 'Can we go too?'

But Archie shook his head. Soon after that the six moved off but not before Ian had seen me and told me to go and pick whelks with Mother. Whelks! That was a slow job if ever there was one! But seeing how I was in disgrace I didn't say anything, just nodded. Even then he gave me a last warning to behave myself. Of course I'd behave myself. What else could I do?

We stood watching till the deputation had disappeared. We could hear them laughing a while after that.

We found our way to the bridge and started throwing stones at a wee bit of wood which had landed on a rock, at least the others threw and I just watched because of my sore hand.

Donald Eoghain, Donald, son of Ewen, was boasting how good he was and telling me he could beat me.

'That's something new then,' said I.

'It is not,' said Hugh of Cat's Cave—these two always backed each other up. 'Donald's much better than you.'

Well, I stuck it for a while and then I thought I'd have a try and I threw three times but missed because of my sore hand.

'Och! you couldn't hit a haystack at ten yards!' shouted Donald. I was angry by this time and sprang at him and we had a wrestle till he kicked my sore foot and I gave a yell and broke free.

'You can't throw and you can't fight!' shouted Hugh, grinning all over his face.

'Fight! I can knock a man down—a full—' but here Archie bumped into me so hard I had to grab the wooden parapet to save myself from falling.

'What are you meaning—' I began when I heard him whisper 'Hold your tongue!'

I swallowed hard and stayed silent. Hugh and Donald went off laughing and jeering up the hill and we were left alone.

I expected Archie to say what he thought of me but he didn't, just leaned against the bar and watched the burn go chuckling and gurgling under the bridge.

'Better take care what you say, Sam,' he said at last straightening up.

'They'll know soon enough!' I pointed out.

'But will they? Nobody knows you knocked him down except you and me.'

'Well, he'll tell, won't he? They'll have the whole story coming home to-night.'

We started walking slowly up the hill and behind us we heard the shouting of the scholars coming out to play.

'Suppose he never got up!' Archie said. It fair took the wind out of me.

'You said yourself he was breathing!'

'Oh aye! breathing—but it was very funny breathing.'

'You're not meaning—not meaning—he'd die?'

'Och! I don't know, Sam, but just suppose—I mean just suppose he never went home then nobody knows but you and me what happened.'

'They all know about the sheep at home—'

'Yes, about the sheep but not about knocking him down.'

'Oh! I never told them that!'

'Well, don't breathe a word to anyone, not a word, mind.'

'Of course I won't. What do you take me for?' and I left Archie at the top of the hill, he to go home and me to go to the beach to pick whelks but even that might be better than being with Archie when he was so low in his spirits.

I crossed over the crofts and joined Mother down at the water's edge.

'We saw them off!' I told her by way of explanation. She had already gathered a pailful.

The tide was still on the ebb so we had plenty of time to fill a few pails. The day was calm and all the movement there was was the swish of a tiny wave as it came in and then drew back. I picked and picked till my fingers were sore. Mother laughed at me when I complained.

'Sore! Oh Sam, you haven't started yet.'

She was used to the work as indeed were all the neighbours for with the money they earned selling whelks they paid for the oatmeal we had to buy. Mother being a widow she had to pick more than most, at least till Ian had grown big enough to go to the fishing.

I took another while at it and then groaned saying my back was sore.

'I'm big enough now, Mother, to go to the east coast fishing and then you won't need to pick whelks.'

She gave me a look then, and not a pleased one I thought.

'You're too young to be talking about the fishing,' she said pushing a stray lock of dark hair out of her eyes. 'Just you work a little harder, Sam, and we'll keep the wolf from the door that way.'

Well, it was a long day but at last the tide came to my rescue lapping round the rocks and covering the whelks. I was off up the bank at a run, not waiting for Mother who had the sack to tie and leave in a rock pool. I made for my grandfather's cottage. I was starving. I'd had nothing since breakfast and that was no more than a memory. When I got near I saw my grandfather on a ladder putting the finishing touches to the new thatch on the roof. Most of us put thatch on at this time of year before the worst of the winter.

'Is that yourself, Sam?' he greeted me, 'and have you been down at the beach? There's a nicely thatched roof for you. It'll keep us warm and dry for another year.' And he patted the thatch lovingly but I was not greatly interested in that work so I ran into the house and told my grandmother that I was starving.

'Well! we'll soon cure that, Sam. Sit you down while I butter you a bannock to be going on with.'

My grandmother was a big woman, near a head taller than grandfather. She had a round rosy face, and had a kind word and a joke for everyone.

'You've been busy all day! Well, wasn't that good! You're a real help to your mother. We saw her on her way down. I'll make the tea ready for her. But what's keeping your grandfather? Catching his death of cold outside there without his jacket on! And will he come in! Oh! no, though I've called him ten times already. There's always something more to be done. Calum could do the roof just as well and maybe better but will he let him!'

If it was my roof I'd let Uncle Calum do it or anyone else who had a mind to and that's a fact, but people are funny about the things they want to do themselves. Now if I could be out with a dog on the hill I wouldn't ask for better.

But presently grandfather came in with my mother.

'They'll just tell the factor we're not going to pay any more rent,' he was saying, 'till we get the hill back. There's no harm in speaking out.'

'But I'm sure there is!' exclaimed Mother. 'Why, father, whoever heard of people talking to factors before?'

'Oh! I don't know so much about that,' he replied gently,

'or if we haven't, then maybe it's time we began.'

They argued the point back and forth while we drank tea, the one making no impression on the other.

'Was it thatching the Queen's palace you were?' my grandmother broke in at last, 'you out there without your jacket, catching your death of cold!'

'I like to see a thing well done!' retorted Grandfather. 'If you can thatch a house as good as that, Sam, when you're a man you'll have something to be proud of!'

'I'm not going to thatch houses! I'm going to be a shepherd out on the hill.'

'Is that so? But I've heard even shepherds have to come home at night!'

'And how is the dog?' grandmother asked me. 'You were very foolish Sam, to let Murdo catch you.'

Now they were going to start scolding once more. Suddenly I remembered Archie.

'Does—does Black Murdo live alone?' I asked. No, they said, he had his mother with him. He was very good to her, yes, for all his faults, he was a good son.

Well, that relieved my mind a little for if Murdo had not gone home there would have been a search party out for him. I told them Ben was fine and then I was seized with impatience to get home and I hurried Mother away. The short winter's day was closing but as we climbed it seemed to grow lighter, for the west was clear and holding on to the last of the daylight.

When we reached the top I hurried ahead. Ben must have been missing me. He used to go everywhere with me. I burst into the house calling to him. It was pitch dark and I groped my way to his corner half afraid he had already gone till my hand came on his back.

'Oh! Ben, it's me. Are you better? Poor Ben. I'll get you food.'

'You make too much of that animal!' The words came out of the darkness and gave me a fright. I hadn't seen

Uncle Donald sitting by the fire, a Bible on his knee.

'He's hurt! I want to make him well.'

'A dog is only a brute beast without a soul! Do not make an idol of him!'

Was he a brute beast without a soul? I didn't know, but I did know he loved me and I was pretty sure that Uncle Donald did not. I got Ben some food and fresh water. He sniffed the food but would not eat in spite of all my coaxing.

Mother came in exclaiming how dark it was.

'Why did you not light the cruisie, Donald? Oh! and you've let the fire out!'

She was down on her knees at once putting the embers together with the tongs, then she fed little bits of peat into them till first smoke spiralled upward and then small flames came throwing huge shadows on the walls. I could see Ben now. He was just lying the same way. He hadn't moved at all and that made my heart sore.

'Run for the cows now, Sam, while I get the dinner.' Cows! Me! After working all day and coming home tired out! Where was the justice in that? Uncle Donald had been in all day. Why couldn't he get the cows? But *he* never did anything unless it was to find fault.

It was quite dark by now and if the cows were lying in the field I'd never see them. However, there they were patiently waiting by the byre chewing the cud. I opened the door and they went in each to her own place and all I had to do was to tie them. Mother came out to milk and I went back in to talk to Ben and tell him why I'd been away all day. He licked my hand with a hot tongue and whined his thanks.

Mother came back saying Betsi was keeping a nice drop of milk and I was to go over to Effie's with a jugful.

'I'm hungry!' I protested, 'I'll go after—'

'Wheest! you can't be hungry after what you ate at your grandfather's. Did you see Effie to-day, Donald?'

She had to repeat the question before he told her that he had not seen the old woman.

'That's not like her! She's usually over to pass the time of day. She can't be feeling well. Tell her I'll be over later, Sam, if she doesn't feel like coming out.'

I took the jug and made my way past the big rowan tree which grew in front of Effie's cottage. The old folk said rowan trees were good for keeping away witches but Effie was very like a witch and the rowan tree hadn't kept her away!

'Anybody in?' I called at the door. The breeze sighed through the bare branches rattling the last of the dead leaves. I heard a shuffling inside and then Effie's old cracked voice crying, 'Come in! Come in! What are you waiting for?'

Well, it was the cats really. Effie had a houseful of them. Now I don't mind cats one at a time like. They're good for keeping rats out of the corn and a cat at the fireside purring is a comfortable sight but when it comes to seven or eight—I was never sure how many—pairs of eyes glowed out of the dark, well, I wasn't just so fond of them then. I stepped warily into the passage where Effie kept her buckets of water and at that very moment the big tiger-striped tom seeing the door open flung himself out and nearly made me spill the milk. Effie tut-tutted.

'Is it afraid of cats you are now? And is it not strange that Tomas cannot stand the sight of you? But if it was Ian coming in that door he'd be purring and rubbing himself to his boots! Ah! it's great the sense some animals have! Well! come in, come in and don't stand there half in and half out and the cold coming in behind you. Put the milk on the dresser and sit down till I get your news.'

All I wanted to do was to go home but that would not have been mannerly so I sat down on the bench and hoped against hope that she would not keep me long. First she wanted to know where we had been all day, not a sight of us from morning to night and herself so bad with her back she could hardly move.

'We were picking whelks all day. I picked four buckets.' Three and a bit would have been nearer the truth but four sounded better.

'Did you now. Well! Well! You're a great help to your mother.'

Now this was just what I thought myself, but there was something about Effie's tone which left me not quite comfortable.

There was a pause and to give myself something to do I counted the cats, three by the fire and one over in a chair and—and—yes, one on the rafters. I could see the glow of its eyes above me. Effie moved a peat on the fire and the flame shot up lighting her old leathery, wrinkled face framed in jet black hair.

Suddenly she spoke again in quite a different voice saying 'Oh! if the little girls were alive, they would be good to their mother. The wee darlings! I can see them yet—the lovely hair they had like gold it was, spun gold. It did my heart good to see them playing out there beside the rowan tree and to think they had to die and lie in the cold grave!'

Her voice had sunk to a whisper. I shivered. My sisters, Mary and Margaret, had taken measles and died within a week of each other when I was a baby. That was what had left such a gap between me and Ian. Mother never spoke of them. Only Effie made them come alive for me by talking of them and the things they did and the way they spoke. I often thought deep down I must be a poor second best, me being red-headed and quick tempered, to the yellow haired girls. To get her off the little girls, I told her about the deputation.

'D E — P U — T A T — I O N .' She stretched the word to immense length—'and what sort of a thing is that? What makes them so bold as to want to talk to Alasdair Ruadh himself?'

I knew it all by now and I rattled it off quite proudly.

Her dark eyes were fixed on my face and gleamed in the firelight.

'Well! Well! is that so? They're hardy, going to Alasdair Ruadh with a speech like that! Are they not afraid they'll be thrown out?'

'Why wouldn't he listen to them?' I asked, half angry. 'Don't you want to get the hill back, Effie?' She did not answer at once but made chewing movements with her jaws.

'And who has sheep to put on the hill? Will you tell me that?'

'Why, we all have a few, most of us anyway—'

'Aye! most of us, most of us, but not poor Effie!'

'You could get a sheep or two,' said I, anxious for everyone to like the plan, 'and they'd breed!' She grinned at that, showing stumps of decaying teeth.

'Oh! aye!' she murmured, 'Oh! aye! you're a good boy and Effie would soon have a flock of sheep.' And she cackled away quietly to herself in a way which made the hair rise at the nape of my neck. I got up and made for the door. Tomas must have changed his mind about the benefit of the night air for he was waiting on the door sill. I grabbed his tail and pulled hard. He let out a yowl and I fled laughing, shaking Effie's antics out of my mind.

I had fallen asleep by the fire long before Ian came home that night but I woke with the stir and saw Mother making him tea and heard her asking were his feet dry. I didn't want to know about his feet but what the factor had said.

'Did he say he'd give us back the hill?' I asked, propping myself up on one elbow. Ian gave a dry kind of a laugh and shook his head.

'There now!' cried Mother, 'what did I tell you! You've made bad worse.'

Ian put down his mug and wiped his mouth with the back of his hand and shook his head again.

'No! he didn't refuse us anything. He wouldn't see us at all.'

'Wouldn't see you!' Mother and I exclaimed together. After all the trouble they had taken polishing their boots and tramping seven to eight miles into the village. That was a shame!

'Why would he not see you, Ian?' Mother asked.

Ian looked first at Mother and then at me in a strange kind of way as if he were seeing us and yet not seeing us. He gave his head a little shake and then said, 'He will talk to tenants and only to tenants. That's what the clerk told us.' He fell silent again both hands round the mug.

'Tenants!' he said suddenly. 'Oh! no, we're not tenants but who pays the rent? If we did not go south every year and earn wages he'd get no rent but we're not worth talking to! The clerk, a wee skinny, scrawny chap, went into the great man's office but he was out again in two-twos to tell us that. Nervous he was too, eyeing us as if he expected us to leap the counter and charge in!'

'Oh! Ian, you didn't act wild?'

Ian gave Mother a long look and then putting down the mug he stretched out his arm and spread the fingers of his right hand, as powerful an arm and hand as was in the whole of the Braes.

'I could have picked him up in one hand,' he said slowly and regretfully, 'and oh! shaken the life out of him no bother at all—but I didn't. No, we were quiet spoken and polite but it was no use. The clerk hurried us to the door just the same.'

Mother gave a sigh of relief.

'You would need to get up very early in the morning to get the better of Alasdair Ruadh.'

But Ian shrugged that off. 'That was just the beginning. We're not finished yet.'

I was aching to know about my own escapade.

'Did—did—they say anything about the sheep?' I forced

myself to ask. He swung round on me.

'Aye they were asking indeed and they're making a cell ready in the jail for you this very minute.'

My heart went down into my boots and I stood there looking very silly.

But Mother told him not to tease me and Ian growled that I'd better get out of his sight then which I did.

I could hear their voices rising and falling in the kitchen until I fell asleep.

3 *Ben*

But days passed and nothing happened and I was getting to the point of thinking that nothing was going to happen at all. But then Archie came up one morning and told me his father wanted to see me.

That meant there was something wrong and what could it be but the sheep?

'Oh! it's the sheep all right,' Archie said, his face as long as a fiddle, 'he's been right mad at me.'

And with that he turned and led the way down the hill taking the short cut down the rocks. His house was long and low and the cattle were housed at the far end. I hesitated at the door watching Archie go in. Then I heard Neil shouting to me to come in so there was nothing for it but to face the music. The room was full, well, it always was because they were a big family from Chrissie, the eldest who was sixteen down to the baby in the cradle.

It was one of the noisiest houses you could be in with everyone talking at once but today when they saw me they all fell silent and this made me feel very uneasy.

Neil, a big, broad shouldered man with a curly brown beard was sitting in his usual seat and his wife, Anna, was busy baking.

'And how are you today, Sam?' Neil asked me, and his wife asked after my mother's health. I stammered out that we were all well and they replied politely that they were glad to hear that.

'Aye! if a man has his health,' mused Neil, 'then he has everything.' And his wife said that was a true word.

Little Ewen came toddling over and lifted his arms. I

picked him up and was glad to feel the small body close to me as I sat wishing Neil would hurry up and let me know the worst.

In course of time he did just that.

'I have a letter here from the factor, Sam. He is saying he has complaints from John Mackay, tenant of the Ben Lee grazing, about boys disturbing the sheep. Aye! I'll read you the bit.' Here he spread out the letter on his broad knee.

'—such behaviour cannot be tolerated. As clerk of the township you are well aware that only three dogs are allowed in any one township, that is one at each end and one in the middle. There is no necessity for any more as they merely disturb the game and cause annoyance to the shooting tenant. The dog caught chasing sheep must be destroyed. The shepherd, Murdo Matheson, will recognise the animal. I shall send the ground officer, Norman Beaton, to Braes shortly to see that this order has been carried out. I have considered whether to remove the families of both boys caught in the act. I shall not do so immediately but if there is any further trouble, no matter how minor, I shall do so without loss of time.'

Neil folded the thick paper which crackled. No one said a word. Neil put the letter behind a dish on the dresser.

'Aye! it was a pity,' he remarked reflectively, 'you and Archie had so little sense.'

I must have looked a bit startled for I was expecting much worse. Then I remembered that Neil had already let fly at Archie and that was enough for him. He was never one to keep a thing up.

But his wife Anna was a different matter altogether. 'It's lucky for you we're getting off so lightly,' she snapped, 'so the sooner you shoot the dog the better.'

It was only then I realised I was in a trap.

I began to tremble and my foot to beat a tattoo on the floor. I pressed down my heel to stop it.

'I won't shoot Ben! I won't.'

B.O.B.   C

'You won't!' shouted Archie's mother coming at me. 'You'd rather see us all out at Whitsun! Is that what you want? Is it? Is it?'

I shrank back from her but still I muttered, 'I won't! I won't!'

'Neil will then! It's his duty as clerk to the township. Neil will shoot him.' She glared at me.

I gazed at Neil imploringly and he answered the look. 'I don't want to shoot another man's dog,' he replied quietly, 'but I'm thinking you'll have to shoot him yourself, Sam, either you or Ian. See now, be reasonable. He had no business to be chasing Murdo's sheep!'

'He wasn't, he wasn't. He never chases sheep on his own. *I* sent him. It wasn't his fault!'

'Aye! you're right there, lad, for it was you sent him. Look at it this way, it's your mother, yes, and this house too that will suffer. If Norman Beaton finds the dog alive it will be notice to quit for the lot of us.'

'Here's a fine fuss about a dog!' cried Anna shrilly. 'Does a dog matter more than children?'

I felt as if a heavy weight were pressing down on me and I could not get out from under. But shoot Ben! No, no, that I could not do nor let anyone else shoot him either.

I put Ewen down and got to my feet.

'I won't let them shoot him. He did no harm. The sheep are strong at this time of year—we only rounded them up—' my words came out in jerks. 'I'll hide him! That's what I'll do.'

'Well and why not?' said Neil, ignoring his wife's protests. 'There's time enough. Norman Beaton won't come this week anyhow.'

I got out of the house somehow, hearing Anna scolding Neil for being soft as I went. I had to be alone and swallow down the sobs which were crowding my throat. Men! To take him out and shoot him! He trusted me. How could I do a thing like that? Or let anyone else do it? I'd shoot

n first. I lay hidden among bushes and sobbed with rage.
 kept away from home all that day afraid they'd know
 my face that something was wrong.

 was on tenterhooks all next day afraid to go far from the
se in case the man Beaton did come but when it grew
 k I knew Ben was safe for another day. I stood at the
 r wondering where to go for a ceilidh. Most nights I
 t to Archie's, us being friends and Neil being a great
 y-teller but I couldn't go there now with Anna mad at
 about the dog.

 ust then my uncle came out. 'Is that you, Sam? I'm
 ng to visit the Master. Will you come with me?'

 Ve all called the schoolmaster 'the Master'. I was sur-
 sed at Donald asking me. He'd never done so before and
 never been in the Master's house. Why it almost made a
 n of me at one go but yet I was never at ease with
 nald and did not know what to say to him as we tramped
 vnhill.

 he Master lived above the school and we reached his
 r by an outside stair. While we waited for the door to
 opened I looked across the sound to Raasay. The moon
 l risen and made a silver path for herself right across the
 to the black rocks below us.

 Norah, the servant, led us in and we walked into a room
 ich seemed to me a blaze of light. I gazed and gazed. It
 ne from the big oil-burning lamp on the dresser. I
 ildn't take my eyes off it, amazed at how steadily the
 :k burned. There was no smell and it made everything as
 ght as day. I hardly heard what the Master and his wife
 re saying I was so taken up admiring the house. My eyes
 re drawn to the fireplace in the wall. All of us had our
 : in the middle of the floor and so there was a lot of
 oke but here there was none. I suddenly noticed that
 rah was giggling at me. She was a silly girl and always
 gling at something when she was in school. Well, I wasn't
 ing to give her any reason to laugh at me by playing

the Johnny Raw. I looked down at the floor and tried
take an interest in what the Master was talking abo
Church matters and the chance of my Uncle Donald be
sent to Rona as a catechist. I wished he'd go.

But then the Master began talking about Ben Lee a
saying it belonged to Lord Macdonald and that he ha
perfect right to do what he pleased with his own propert
looked at my uncle wondering if he would say Ben Lee l
always belonged to us. But, no, he agreed with the Mas
I thought that very strange when his father and brother w
on the other side. The Master began telling us how go
this Lord Macdonald's father had been to the Skye peop
building roads and bridges and piers.

'If it were not for him,' he said turning to me, 'you wo
have no good things coming up from the south in shi
luxuries our forefathers never dreamed of! Sugar and
and fancy goods of every description!'

We bought sugar and tea right enough and I tried hard
think what fancy goods we got but I still hadn't thou
of anything when the Master's wife cut me a huge slice
dumpling and gave me a cup of very sweet tea. She w
kind-hearted although she did think the gentry had
right to trample all over us. I sat chewing the dumpling a
wishing I could argue with the Master. Why was it such
crime not to pay rent? He talked a lot about the Irish do
this and now we were copying the Irish. Well, I'd nev
seen an Irishman in my grandfather's house. I don't thi
he knew any. Still I enjoyed the dumpling and the tea an
noticed that Norah got skim milk and that put me one up.

We left at last. It was good to be on the move and t
wind fresh in my face. It had been hot as an oven inside.

Donald began talking. I thought he'd be tired of it
he had been at it all evening but no he was off again. T
Master, he told me, was a man of great learning and I wo
do well to heed his words.

'Should I heed his words more than grandfather's?' I aske

'Your grandfather is a good man,' he said slowly, 'but in this one matter he is being led astray by agitators.'

So it was agitators now! It had been Irishmen before.

'I don't know any agitators. I never see any in his house just the neighbours and they all think the way he does. Since the old factor promised them the hill back we ought to get it.'

Out of doors and away from the intimidating presence of my old schoolmaster with his long words and slow speech and weighty arguments I felt quite easy keeping my end up with Donald.

'There is nothing in writing! It is just fancy! They delude themselves.'

I stopped and faced him. 'How do *you* know? It happened ages ago and you'd only be a boy but grandfather was a man and of course he'd remember every word the old factor said.'

Donald flushed up and clenched his fists and for a minute I thought he was going to strike me. I was glad to see him in a temper. It made him more human somehow but then he sighed and began to argue once more, so feeling that I had had the best of it I ran off. I was anxious to get home and see how Ben was.

I went as fast as I could and arrived quite out of breath.

Mother was in and Effie by the fire with Tomas on her knee.

I boasted that Uncle Donald couldn't keep up with me and added that the Master didn't want us to get the hill back. Mother gave me a look which meant 'Effie's here'. Effie herself gave one of her usual cackles of laughter. 'Get the hill back! Alasdair Ruadh won't give you the hill back!'

What got me was that she sounded so pleased about it as if a victory for Alasdair Ruadh was a victory for *her*. I was just going to argue when I looked in the corner and Ben wasn't there.

'Mother! Where's Ben?' I thought for a moment she might have moved him to make him more comfortable but she started and peered into the corner and then shook her head saying, 'Oh! he's gone.'

And suddenly I thought I understood the whole thing.

'You let him out! You let him out!'

'No, indeed, Sam, I did not. Why would I do a thing like that?'

'You did, you did and Ian shot him. That's it, that's what happened. You got me out of the way between you, you got me out of the way and then Ian—' but I could not say it a second time. The words wedged themselves in my throat and in a second or two I'd burst out weeping but at that moment Donald came in and so I turned in fury on him.

'It was a trick, just a trick. All of you, you were all in it. *You* asked me to go down to the Master's—and you never asked me to go anywhere with you before but you knew I'd never let Ian shoot—shoot—him so you got me away! He was my dog—my dog—'

'Now, Sam, you know fine we did nothing of the sort and that's no way to speak to your uncle.'

But I was lost to all reason and beat my fists on Donald's chest shouting, 'You deceived me, you cheated me! I hate you! I hate you!'

My uncle struggled with me and he was much stronger than he looked but I was in such a passion I believe I could have stood up to Ian himself. I heard Effie saying, 'Here's a fine fuss about a dog. I didn't know they were so scarce! Why would Ian shoot it? Was it killing sheep?'

I missed Mother's reply because I had torn myself free and shoving Donald aside I ran out.

I ran without thinking just to get away from them all but then I took a thought to myself and halted. If Ian really had shot him he wouldn't have carried the body far at this time of night. He'd have left it on the dung hill or in the stack yard. I turned back and searched all round the house d byre but there was nothing there.

I remembered grandfather's words that if Ben knew he
s dying—and dogs did know—then he'd get out somehow
die where no one would see him. And yet I could not
ogether believe it and went searching all the places
.ere we used to go together calling 'Ben! Ben!' and
.istling when my voice failed. But it was no good. For all I
ew my voice might be reaching him where he lay
ing but he would not answer.

I turned back home. I hardly knew what I was doing. I
.od at length on the moor above our croft and the cold
onlight fell on thatched roofs and on the bare branches of
e rowan tree.

I was making you a den,' I said aloud. 'I was making you
len and they wouldn't have found you. You'd have been
right with me.'

All was bright and cold and empty as I went home.

4 Rent Day

As rent day drew near Mother became more and m
nervous. Ian grew impatient and so she stopped talking
front of him but I had to listen to her fears and to
troubles which she was sure would fall upon us if
Braes men would not pay rent.

The least of these was the doubling of the rent and
worst being turned out.

'They can't do that,' I kept saying, 'if we all stick togeth
I was well up in all the arguments by this time hear
them every night in Neil's house. I wanted her to come w
me and hear them for herself but she would not. Ian a
I were sure that Uncle Donald was doing his best to
her to pay her rent and we were afraid she might. Howe
she did not speak of going to Portree so we became more ea
on that score.

One evening, however, I came in to find her stuffing co
into her pocket. She gave a gasp and then said 'Oh! i
only you, Sam.'

'Did you think it was Ian?' I asked and then rushed
'Mother! you're *not* to pay the rent.'

She straightened her skirt and gave her hair a pat ir
place before she spoke. 'Who said I was going to?'

I pointed to her pocket.

'Oh! that—I'm going to the shop.'

I wanted to believe her but I could not. No one took go
coins to the wee shop which sold tea and tobacco.

'I'll come with you then,' was all I said. 'It's getting la
and you don't like walking in the dark.'

'Are you not going to Archie's?' said she wrapping

plaid round her and not meeting my eye. 'You haven't been there for a while.'

'I can go another night.' I replied and went out with her. The night was dark for the moon was in its last quarter and had not yet risen but I was good in the dark and Mother followed where I led. When we had gained the road a hail shower hit us coming from a cloud as black as ink overhead.

'There now!' exclaimed my mother. 'Why did you come? You'll be soaked.'

As if that mattered! I had more on my mind than a few hailstones even if they did sting my face and bare legs.

'It's only a shower,' I replied, 'and it's clearing behind already.'

I was keeping straight on for the shop when Mother called me back.

'We'll go to your grandfather's. I won't bother with the shop to-night.'

I was pleased to hear this but I pretended otherwise.

'We can go to the shop first seeing we've got this far and—'

But no, she'd go to grandfather's. She had me fair puzzled. Was she meeting someone in the shop who would take her money to the factor? But that didn't make sense because if she was looking for a messenger she had Donald beside her and he'd take it quick enough.

We came to grandfather's house and it was grand to be inside. They put me near the fire to dry off and I sat steaming like a kettle on the boil and old Tweed came close to have his ears pulled and his back stroked.

Mother and the old people talked of this and that but I had a feeling there was something special she wanted to say. At last when Uncle Calum had gone out she came round to it.

'Are you going to Portree tomorrow, Father?' Grandfather said yes, they were all going, it was rent day.

'Then,' said she hurriedly, 'will you pay my rent for me?'

'What nonsense are you talking, girl?' grandmother cried out, 'You know fine we're paying no rent!'

But grandfather kept cool and only said no, he wasn't paying her rent nor his own.

At this Mother argued and pleaded. When they would not agree she wrung her hands. I felt quite ashamed that she should behave like this.

'We'll be put out! That's all that will happen. They'll have the Law on us.'

'We're in this all together, Mhairi,' grandfather repeated, 'and they won't put forty-four men into prison. Well, how could they? The prison in Portree wouldn't hold us!'

'You're only laughing at me! There's many another prison and that's where it will end. Oh! it's all right for you,' she said turning angrily on grandmother, 'you've got a husband to look after you but I have no one and if I lose the croft—'

And at this grandfather looked stern and told her to be quiet, that was wild talk. 'Have you not Ian? Is he not a good son to you? And will Sam not be a good son to you very soon?'

If I'd been asked I'd have claimed I was that already.

After that Mother became more cheerful and before we left she took the gold coins out of her pocket and handed them over to grandfather.

'Keep them for me,' she said. 'They'll be safer with you and I'll start saving for next year's rent.'

They set off next morning, all the tenants of the three townships, Peinchorran, Balmeanach, and Gedintailor, dressed in their Sunday clothes, their Kilmarnock bonnets on their heads.

Archie and I and the rest watched them march off, their heavy boots crunching on the snow which lay thin on the ground. What they were planning was something quite new and we all felt it.

was wondering how to get through the day till they
home with the news in the evening but that was
led for me.

adn't been long back at the house when a man pushed
ithout so much as a by your leave.

ave you a dog?' he demanded.

y mother looked at him. 'No, no, we have no dog.'

Ve'll soon see about that!' and he searched the whole
e looking under the beds and in the back closet, throw-
ur clothes down on the floor and leaving them there.

e came back into the kitchen. 'There's none here,' he

hat's what I told you in the first place,' Mother replied
she spoke so coolly I felt proud of her.

ye! so you did but maybe he's outside, eh! answer
hat!' and he poked his face close to her but Mother went
nitting quite as if there had been nobody there.

Vell! I'm going to see,' he said loudly, 'you don't need to
k you can fool me.' He grabbed me by the upper arm,
hing my skin. If Ben had lived, I thought, he'd have
outside right enough and in a place where you would
find him.

ut in the sunshine I had a good look at the fellow. He
a small man with a thick nose between two flabby
ks and small watery eyes.

e told me to search the byre, making me move every-
g that was in it except the cows. I lifted creels, herring
es and even the pony's harness.

ood life!' said I, 'is it a day old pup you're looking
?' Well! he grabbed me by the ear and pulled and I gave
ll.

ou keep a civil tongue in your head!' he shouted, 'and
vhat I say. Look in that stall now!'

o I pushed past Betsi and looked in the manger. When
me out he was looking up into the rafters and I wished
n would do its droppings in his eye.

He gave in at last and stood in the doorway looking
The sun had disappeared and more snow was beginnin
fall. It was very cold and I was wishing he'd move and
me get back indoors but he hadn't finished yet.

'You had a dog all right,' he said slewing round to w
me, 'you had a dog and you chased Black Murdo's shee
now you tell me where he is. What have you done v
him?'

I suppose it would have been easy to say he'd died
yet I could not bring myself to tell him. I didn't w
Murdo to know his kick had finished Ben. I set my teeth
muttered I had no dog.

For a moment I thought he was going to come at me
there wasn't room to dodge but all of a sudden he seer
to lose interest. A flurry of snow came in the door
he shook himself and said, 'I wonder would your mother h
a cup of tea? It's going to be a cold walk back to Portree.
if I cared! I only hoped he'd be stuck in a blizzard. I follo
him slowly towards the house hoping that Mother wc
refuse him. But would she? She always gave hospitality
strangers. I waited at the side of the house and in no tim
all I saw him come out and make off in a hurry.

I found Mother putting the house to rights.

'You didn't give him any tea?'

'Now, Sam, how could I,' she said pausing in her w
to face me, 'and the kettle empty and the fire black out!'

And sure enough it was!

'The kettle was on the boil when he came in and the
bright.'

'Was it so? Well, the water in the kettle must h
poured itself over the fire. Wasn't that a pity now and
poor fellow thirsty!'

We burst out laughing and it was a joke with us fo
long time how the kettle had emptied itself into the
rather than make tea for Norman Beaton, the ground offic

Talking over his visit afterwards with Archie it str

me he had never mentioned Murdo being knocked down.

'Well, didn't I tell you he wouldn't,' was all Archie would say. 'Would Murdo boast of it?' He was never one to waste words, not like his father who could make a story out of catching a haddy.

As indeed he did out of their visit to the factor. We could get nothing out of grandfather except that the factor told them they had given themselves an extra walk for they would still have to come in with the rent. It was as dull as one of the Master's geography lessons. But when we went to Neil's that evening we found him in full spate.

'Six of us went in,' he was saying, 'just six and the rest waited outside. There he was behind his huge desk in that room full of books, books right along the wall and up to the ceiling and all on Law! Aye, Sam, my boy, if they can't catch you one way they'll catch you another. Well, your grandfather, he was the spokesman. But wait you, I'm taking this too fast. For first Alasdair Ruadh had to have a word with each of us. Oh! that was always his way. He told your grandfather he was looking younger than ever and asked me was I making poetry, all very friendly and pleasant like but mark you, Sam, it's when a person speaks you smooth that you have to be most on your guard. Well, then, he pulled the big rent roll towards him. It looks like the book of judgement where they have all our names and we must answer on the last day—and he ran his finger down the list.

'Ah! yes, here we are, Alasdair Finlayson, Balmeanach, nine pounds eight shillings and eleven pence, and he looked up keeping his finger at the name. Well, your grandfather just stood there, Sam, not saying a word and mighty uncomfortable we all felt. Was he going to fail at the very last? No, no, I didn't believe it but I was wishing he'd speak up and get it over with. The clerk, Neil Grant, had his pen at the ready and still your grandfather kept silent.

'Alasdair Ruadh repeated the sum a bit louder thinking

maybe Alasdair was getting hard of hearing and at that your grandfather gave a little cough and spoke out saying, "Yes, Mr Macdonald, nine pounds eight shillings and eleven pence is the rent for my croft as well I know and I have paid it faithfully all those years since I took over from my father when he died a young man. It was the same sum he paid, yes, and his father before him but they had the grazings of Ben Lee. We have no grazing there and still the same rent was laid upon us. Not one of us could be paying it from what we get from the croft but we go away to earn money and when we are too old our sons go in our place and that is how we manage year after year to pay you but now we want the hill back and then we shall pay the rent!"

'I could see the colour rising in Alasdair Ruadh's face. He has plenty of colour at the best of times but now it got purplish and he clenched the hand which lay on the table and we knew we were in for trouble.

'He turned away from Alasdair and asked each of us in turn but we all said the same thing. I stood there thinking he'd burst out at us and quite prepared for it because he's a hot tempered man and it would have done him good. But he just sat there staring coldly at us and the room as quiet you could hear the breath coming out of us and the creak of our boots as we shifted our weight. Well, I'm telling you that was the worst bit of the whole day. Strange, isn't it? He was just sitting there but I was going hot and cold and wishing myself out of that room. But at last he told us we'd be evicted and that didn't surprise us, we knew he'd say it. "You will be evicted for non-payment of rent." But Alasdair Bàn spoke up once more. Oh! quite calm and courteous. It did my heart good to hear him. He told the factor we were not refusing to pay rent. We had it put by and we would pay as soon as we got Ben Lee which Fear a' Choire promised us we would get.

'At that the rage got the better of him and he banged his fist on the table and shouted at your grandfather, "What

.sense is this? I have been eight years factor to Lord
:donald and my father was ten years factor before that
we have never seen any document setting out any such
mise."

"I do not know about documents," replied your grand-
ter carefully. "Maybe there is no document but between
ourable men there is no need for that." Here the factor
back his head and laughed, but not a real laugh. It
ted on my ears. "In Law," says he, "there must always be
uments, always, always. You have been misled. There
to chance of you getting the hill back. We have a good
ant paying a hundred and thirty pounds for it. Which
you could pay that?" Faced with such a question sudden
: none of us wished to be the first to speak.
He looked from one to the other and laughed again. "You
! You know well enough you cannot pay any such sum.
! enough of this nonsense; you must bring the rent. All
i have got for this day's work is another long walk!" And
t was it and out we went.
But I was proud of your grandfather!'

5 The Tree

I longed to go herring fishing but Ian kept telling me I
too young and hadn't the strength for it.

Well, just at this time grandfather had a touch of lumb
and Calum had a heavy cold so Ian told me to come al
I could hardly believe my luck and went rushing after
chattering with excitement till he told me to take it easy
find it cold, hard work.

Funny the things people say! As if I would!

There was just the three of us, Ian and Seumas, a ne
bour of grandfather's, and me. We should have been four
with other boats all going out we couldn't find a fourth.

It was frosty and the stars bright when we went out to
the net. When that was done we came ashore for an hou
two's sleep at grandfather's. I felt as if I'd only been slee
ten minutes when Ian was shaking me by the shoulde
stumbled down the beach to the coble. We pushed her
and rowed to the *Mary Ann*, anchored in the bay.

'Will there be a lot of herring, Ian?' I was beginning
feel the excitement coming back now that I was truly awa

'I can't tell you,' said my brother, 'but we'll soon see.'

'Ian is getting as good as the "bodach",' Seumas t
me, 'and if the net is full you'll have to show your stren;
Sam, lad.'

We came on the net and with the weight of it the thre
us could hardly pull it aboard.

'Heave! Heave!' cried Seumas. At that I put out ev
ounce of strength I had in me and the herring came
cading into the boat like a waterfall in spate.

We sat back admiring our catch. 'Good life, Sam, you

brought us luck,' said Seumas. Maybe he was just kidding me but I believed him and sat there as proud as a peacock, my chest swelling. It was lucky for us there was a klondyker lying in the narrows of Scalpay for besides being much nearer us than Portree she gave a fair price.

It was still dark when we got back to Balmeanach with not a light anywhere. I wondered how Ian could find the coble but find her he did. I had been getting cold but rowing the coble ashore and pulling her up the beach cured me of that.

They divided the few herring we hadn't sold. 'Take these home, Sam,' said Ian.

'Aren't you coming?' I asked.

'Not just now. I've got things to see to. I'll get a bite at grandfather's.' He had his back to me putting supports to the side of the coble.

'I'll come with you.'

'No, be off with you. Mother will want to know how the fishing went.'

So she would, of course, and I'd be the first to tell her. I took the hill at a run. When I had climbed level with Archie's house I gave it a look. Here I was out all night and him in his bed! I'd have a story for him later and I'd make sure Chrissie was about when I told it. She was about the bossiest girl I knew but now that I could earn money at the fishing she'd have to change her tune.

Thinking about Chrissie I reached the top and cut across the bare fields rimed with frost. I suddenly noticed something moving near the dyke. Had one of the cows got out? I had tied them properly, hadn't I? Ian would be mad at me if they'd eaten the potatoes.

But this thing wasn't the shape of a cow, no, it was a man. But a moment later I saw I was wrong. It was Maggie, Effie's daughter.

'Oh! is that you, Maggie?' I exclaimed, 'I've been out fishing and we got a great catch and we sold four cran to the klondyker over at Scalpay. Wasn't that great?'

She stood staring at me, at least I think she was staring at me for it was so dark I couldn't be sure. I wondered she did not speak. But then she did, each word coming out like a bit of ice.

'Fishing! You! You're too young for that! You're too small to pull your weight in a boat.'

Small! She could not have hit on anything I minded more than to be called small.

'I—I—I'm no—not—small!' I stuttered, 'well, maybe I'm not *tall*, not yet but I—I—I'm strong and can pull as good as a man.'

'As good as a very weak man, I dare say,' she retorted and with that she walked past me making for her own house.

I stood there trembling with anger. To call me small! Small! I'd been meaning to give her half the herring, I had indeed, but now I wouldn't give her as much as a head, the nasty, cross, dried-up stick that she was.

She had me quite upset and I hurried home. I could smell the peat smoke and when I went in there was the fire burning just waiting for the herring to go in the pan and cook in their own fat.

Lovely they were, the best I'd ever tasted and I told Mother the whole history of the night's doings. I came to Maggie last.

'Dear me, she's early,' said Mother. 'I never knew her come in the dark before. She'll be tired, poor girl. You'd better run over with some of the herring later on, Sam.'

Me go over with herring! Not likely. I wouldn't go near the place till Maggie had gone but Mother only laughed and said that her bark was worse than her bite. She'd go over herself some time.

The warmth after the cold night was making me sleepy and I stretched out on the wooden settle and fell fast asleep.

When I woke it was dark and I wondered hazily where

I was. There was a blanket on top of me and an old coat doubled up under my head. I'd been dreaming I was still in the *Mary Ann* and the ripple and plash of the bow wave were still sounding in my ears. I yawned and stretched. Mother must have gone out for she had smoored the fire. I lay wondering whether to get up and light the cruisie but remembering the stink of fish oil I wrinkled my nose. I remembered the beautiful lamp in the Master's house with its blue bowl for the paraffin, its long, elegant funnel and round white globe. I'd get one for Mother, that's what I'd do with the first money I earned. I'd go to Portree and then I'd carry it home carefully. Wouldn't she be pleased and proud! But if I was to earn money I'd have to get them to take me out fishing a few times and at that I sprang up and hurried out to be met on the doorstep with a buffet of wind. I put my head down and made straight for my grandfather's.

The house was full of people as indeed it generally was of a winter's evening. I got a great welcome. I'd brought luck to the boat.

'Are you better, grandfather?' I asked, 'or will I go out for you tonight as well?'

They all laughed—I don't know why—but that's the way when you say something serious.

'Is it wanting rid of me you are?' teased grandfather, 'but you'll have to learn your trade first. The wind's too strong for fishing the night.'

I argued the point. There was only a breeze but Uncle Calum cut me short. 'She's backing. Calm one minute and a squall tearing down the next. That's the worst kind of wind, not one that blows fair.'

My grandmother set down a plate of salt herring and potatoes in front of me and told me I had been a great help. She asked where Mother was.

'I think she went over to Effie's,' I said. 'Maggie's back from Portree.'

'She's a good walker, is Maggie,' said grandmother settling down to knit. 'She was telling me once she leaves the village at ten o' clock and is home at noon.'

The rest agreed that she was a good walker, as good as a man any day yes, and a good worker. She was a servant in the fiscal's house and they thought the world of her there.

With my mouth half full I said she hadn't left Portree at ten because I'd met her when I was on my way home from the fishing.

And on that there was a sudden hush in the crowded room. The silence made me look up. Grandmother had stopped knitting, grandfather left off filling his pipe, Calum stopped coughing and everyone was looking at me. What had I said to cause such a stir?

'Where did you meet her, Sam? Take your time and tell us just what happened.' This was grandfather speaking. For the life of me I couldn't see why he should look so serious and as to taking time why I hadn't spent more than a minute in Maggie's company. It was all quite simple but all the same I found myself stammering as I was apt to do when nervous. I told them how I had met her.

'Yes, yes, and what did she say, Sam? Did she say why she was so early?'

'No, no, she didn't. I told her I'd been fishing and she and she—'

'Well?'

'She (why must I say it?) she said I was too small.'

Then they nodded their heads. 'She was mad at the boy!'

'So she was because he'd seen her! That's plain as the hand before your face.'

Grandmother came alive and broke a peat over her knee.

'We'd be blind if we didn't see it!' she said, 'she was taking her spite out on the boy!'

But why should she? What had I done to her?

Everyone was in this except me.

'Send for the Peinchorran men,' they said, 'we must be

all in this together.'

Now I saw a chance of getting into things myself.

'I'll go, grandfather, I'll run fast. What shall I tell them?'

But he only smiled and shook his head gently. Two men went out without a word said.

I felt something like a shiver up my spine. Something strange was happening. No one sat at ease, everyone was tense, ready for action.

Well, I wasn't going to ask how Maggie could harm us. Why should she want to? Mother always shared anything she had with Effie and looked after her when she was sick. I puzzled and puzzled inside my head but it was like looking for landmarks in a thick mist.

I had begun the day—and it felt like weeks away now —feeling myself a man among men but now I was right back where I started, ignored by my elders, too young and ignorant to be let into a secret.

I had finished eating by the time Calum came in to say the Peinchorran men had come. Out they all went silently, me at the tail.

Off they went up hill. The wind came down at us, pouncing like a wild beast and then hurling itself out to sea. It was taking me all my time to keep up and it was only when we had gained the top that I noticed the group had spread out. I had only one man in front of me. They had thinned into a long line.

I was close to home now and one bit of me would have liked to slink in and cower under the blankets but another bit of me was determined to see this thing out.

We were past my home and had surrounded Effie's.

'Ready! At it, boys.' I heard an axe hit wood. Were they breaking down Effie's door? Why should they? It was never locked. If they wanted to go in they had only to lift the latch. Then in the gloom I saw a man bringing his axe down on the rowan tree. I was amazed. The rowan tree! It was *my* tree. I had climbed up its trunk and into most of its branches. I had made myself a house in it and had fallen out of it many times. I had watched its tight flower heads spread into white pancakes of blossom every May and seen it covered in bright red berries every autumn. What harm had the tree done them?

The men took it in turns. No one spoke. We listened in silence to the sound of the axe strokes. The tree began to quiver. The axe had bitten into the trunk all round. They flung a rope up into the branches, caught the end and pulled all together. With a sharp crack like gun-shot the trunk broke and lurching sideways scattered the men from its path.

'What are you doing to my tree?'

'We are breaking your tree now but we shall break down your house next if you send rent to the factor, Effie Uisdein.'

'Send rent!' her voice rose, 'I am sending no rent!'

'Is your daughter in the house?'

'She is.'

'Ask her why she came so early in the morning?'

'She came to see her old mother! She is a good girl.'

'Tell her to go back empty-handed. If she carries the rent or the half of it there will be no roof over your head when she comes back.'

The wind came down from Glamaig in a sudden squall.

'I am not sending any rent!' I heard Effie wail when it was passed but no one answered. They had gone.

6 *The Factor Moves*

Archie was leaning on the lower half of the byre door and watching Flossie's pup circling the hens. She had them packed neatly in a tight group and if one so much as moved a foot, the puppy snaked towards it and the hen hastily rejoined its fellows.

'See that!' said Archie. His voice broke the spell, the pup came bounding over to leap up on him and the hens went off indignantly cackling as if they had escaped a great danger.

Archie rubbed his hands. 'She's going to be good, Sam!'

Well, I wasn't going to deny she might but I wasn't going to lavish praise on her either. She was one of the smooth coated kind like her mother, she had a thin wisp of a tail and she wriggled so much when she got excited I thought she'd end up choking on her own tail.

'If you like I'll keep her for you!'

'I don't like bitches.' I wasn't really cross but looking at this pup made me remember Ben. I could see him so plainly looking at me, ears cocked, one paw in the air a way he had when he was waiting orders.

'Hugh was saying he'd like her.'

'Hugh!' I snorted, 'they haven't even got a croft. It would be a pity to waste a good dog on the likes of him.'

Archie gave me a look and I expect he knew I'd take her in the end but we didn't say any more at the time. Archie went back to cleaning the byre and I sat down on an upturned bucket. I could hear Archie's brothers and sisters shouting away at each other through in the house. There was such a lot of them that if they wanted to be heard they had to shout. I was still turning over in my mind the events of the night before.

'If Maggie had taken the rent what would have happened?' I asked.

'They'd be hoping the factor would turn you out and give them your croft.'

This fairly staggered me. 'But Effie can't even work her own! It's Ian that does all the ploughing and the harvesting too and I have to herd her cow as well as our own!'

'I know but if she had two crofts she'd get a husband for Maggie and they do say Black Murdo is courting her.'

Black Murdo!

I didn't like the sound of this one bit and I sat staring at Archie. Maybe I wouldn't have been so amazed if it had been someone else who was to lose his croft. I couldn't believe people would treat *us* so badly. Archie stopped working and leaned on the graip.

'But I don't know, would two crofts do it?' he said seriously. 'Maggie has a temper and then he'd have the old woman on his back as well!'

Even to talk of it made me shudder.

'I wouldn't live with those two for six crofts,' I said firmly.

'You see,' Archie went on. 'They're looking for a weak person to give in and the widows are as likely as any, well, not your mother of course but Effie here and there's Kate Mhoir in Peinchorran. If they paid the rent then others would follow.'

I winced when he mentioned Mother for she would have paid at one time. Not now though and I blessed Norman Beaton for stiffening her resolution by his rudeness.

'They're seeing about Kate Mhoir,' Archie added, matter of fact.

'She hasn't got a tree!'

'No, but they're keeping an eye on her and if she goes to Portree someone will go with her.'

'I'll keep an eye on Effie!' I said just as Chrissie came through from the house.

She gave one of her shrill laughs that got on my nerves.

'You keep an eye on Effie! You're never there to keep an eye on anything! Wandering about like a dog without a master!'

I fired up at this. Me not keeping an eye! If it hadn't been for me Maggie would have been off with the rent and no one any the wiser. If I hadn't been out fishing—

'Och! we've heard enough about your fishing. It was just the once you were out. To listen to you you'd think you'd been one of the crew for months.'

'Well! so I shall be soon.'

'Oh! no, you're too small.' I jumped up from my seat and was after her. She made one dash for the house calling to Archie to bring in peats.

'Let her get her own peats! Come on, let's go down to the shore and look for corks.'

When I went home that evening the first person I met was Uncle Donald. Ever since that night at the schoolmaster's he'd been going out of his way to talk to me. He didn't mention the land troubles now but he would ask me what I wanted to be and so on. I knew very well what I wanted to be—a shepherd but I was not going to tell him so I said—just to keep him quiet—that I'd go to sea and maybe some day I'd be a captain and have a ship of my own. He'd smile at that and say I'd have to go back to school to learn navigation.

'But whatever you become, Samuel,' he would say, 'you must obey your earthly superiors in all things. As a sailor you must obey the captain and the mate and everyone above you but at the same time you must remember to keep your real concern for spiritual matters and for the life eternal. We are only on this earth for a short time but we shall be for ever and ever in Heaven or in Hell!'

Well, I didn't like the way he looked at me out of his

pale eyes and I'd remember all the things I'd done wrong so the upshot was that if I saw him coming I'd hide quick and to make sure he wasn't in I'd go round the back of the house to where there was a tiny window in the thatch and I'd have a look through. Sometimes he'd be keeping family prayers so then I'd put my ears to a wee hole I had made and I'd have an idea whether he was near the end or not. However this night I walked straight into him on the doorstep.

'Is it you, Samuel? I was hoping you'd come. I'm just on my way to visit the Master and I'm sure he'd welcome you too.'

I hesitated trying to think up some excuse. I wasn't going, I was sure of that. I'd get a better supper, but I'd have to listen to all that talk about how good the landlord was and so I'd do without the supper. But I couldn't think what to say.

It was then he gave a sort of false laugh and said, 'I'm sure there will be plum duff.'

Plum duff! Was I so set on my stomach that I'd go anywhere to get plum duff?

'I don't want plum duff,' I said stiffly, and walked past him into the house. After that he stopped bothering about me.

When fine weather came in March we were all busy cutting wrack at low tide and hauling it up above high water mark. Ian had the job of taking the dried seaweed from the shore right up to our croft. Sally, our black pony, carried two creels slung one on each side of the pack saddle.

Dragging wet seaweed up the beach was a slow sort of a business but we boys had a bit of fun from time to time chasing each other into pools and trying to put crabs down one another's back.

I had to help Ian load the creels and it was not easy to get exactly the same weight on each side. We were lucky to have a pony though for many of the women were carrying loads on their own backs up the steep green bank to their crofts. The women laughed to see me gazing at them.

'See how strong the Braes women are, Sam! You'll need to get one for a wife and then you won't need a pony!'

I blushed and they laughed so I was glad when Mother complained of being thirsty and told me to go to the well at Cat's Cove and bring her a jugful of water, for Angus's well had the best water in the parish.

I ran off delighted to get clear of the wrack for a while. I crossed the neck of land which we call Aird and came down on the sand at the far side. Here the bay was open to the north. I liked the feel of the sand under my toes and I ran along close to the water's edge where the little white waves came in one after the other with a kind of sigh or whisper. Going like the wind I was soon close to Angus's cottage. It was built just above high water mark and to protect it from storms Angus had built a dyke in front. By building his house here he did not need to pay rent. He had no croft and no animals but earned his living fishing. We boys envied his son Hugh because when we all had to work hard he could do just as he fancied.

There was no sign of Hugh but when I reached the well I saw Jean, Hugh's sister, there before me.

'Well, Sam,' she said smiling up at me, 'are you not the big stranger? Where have you been hiding yourself? Hugh's wearying for a sight of you.'

I was surprised to hear that, for Hugh and I were not too fond of each other but I only asked where he was.

He had gone over to Raasay with his father to get sea-weed for Archie's father. He was the lucky one. I wished I could go to Raasay too. I told her my errand and she said Mother was right. They had the best water for miles around.

'Is this not a pretty place, Sam?' she said then and of course I agreed because she was the prettiest girl in Braes with her dark, curly hair, rosy red cheeks and a smile to win your heart. In a way it was hard to believe that Chrissie and she were both girls.

'Yes, indeed, much better than up on that high moor of yours!' But this was going too far.

'It's bonny up on the moors with the larks singing and the heather in bloom and the bees humming over it.'

'The heather's not long in bloom,' she countered with a flash of her white teeth, 'and we have sandpipers and oyster-catchers and the—'

'They don't sing!'

She gave a little laugh. 'I know they don't but all the same—I don't know how it is—I love hearing them. It's a sad call but do you know this, Sam, I keep remembering it when I'm away in the city and I hear it in my dreams, and when I wake I feel like weeping because I'm far away and all I hear is the rattle of the dust carts over the cobbles.'

We sat in silence a wee while till she said she'd get me a piece. I waited patiently till I saw her coming back but this time she had two little girls clinging to her skirt. From this shelter they peered out at me and I made faces to amuse them. The bigger one was clutching a small wooden doll.

'Why, Ian had a doll in his pocket just like that one the time he came back from Portree with the Deputation!'

'Oh!' was all she replied and for some reason not at all clear to me she looked put out, then she added, 'Oh! yes, Widow Stewart keeps a stock of them in her wee shop on the corner and they only cost a penny and lots of people buy them.'

'I expect they do,' I agreed munching the piece she had given me, my eyes on the doll and then I noticed something. 'Look at that! It's got a nick on its head just like the one Ian had.'

'Oh! well, maybe a lot of them have,' Jean answered vaguely, 'a knife could slip.'

I thought about that. I supposed it was just possible but now one of the little girls piped up 'En gave Ina dolly!'

En? Who was En? I never heard of anyone with that name. And then I suddenly understood what she meant.

Ian, of course and she couldn't make two of it. 'I—an' so
she said En. But what had Jean been talking about? I looked
at her and saw that she was red all over her face and neck.

'If your mother's thirsty you'd better be getting back.'
And without another word she took to her heels with the
two little ones crying after her like lambs after their mother.

She was in a great hurry all of a sudden! She hadn't said
a word about Mother being thirsty till the wee one had
given the game away! Why did she have to make such
a mystery about the doll if Ian did give it. Why didn't she
just say so? But why would Ian go and give *them* a doll?
They were not related to us. Now *I* had wanted a knife and
was still wanting it!

Puzzling over the matter I got back with the water and
not long afterwards the tide covered the tangle so we walked
up to grandfather's. Sally was already there at the side of
the house, her head hanging and the sweat matting her
rough coat.

We went in and at once I sensed that something had
happened. Both Ian and Calum were in and grandfather had
a letter in his hand.

'What is it?' said Mother. 'Is it from the factor?'

They nodded. Ian had just finished reading it aloud.

'They'll put us out!' said Mother, all her fears back
again.

I looked from face to face feeling both frightened and
excited. The deputation and the rent day which was no
rent day now seemed far away and I'd begun to think
nothing was going to happen at all. But now here it was.

Mother continued to complain till grandmother turned
on her sharply 'There's only five names in that letter: your
father, your brother, Calum, Donald and James Nicolson and
Peter Macdonald! It's for me to complain and for Peter's
young wife! But your name is not here at all so why start
crying before you are hurt?'

This shamed Mother into silence but I do not think she was

easier in her mind. We all looked at grandfather. He was the one who could tell us what to do. But he was in no hurry to say anything. He sat with the pipe in his hand looking at it but not seeing it. Then he looked up and saw us and smiled, 'We've got a fortnight. He's still thinking we'll pay the rent but we won't. No, this time it's different, there's not going to be any evicting. We won't let the sheriff officer give us the papers and we'll be all in it together, not just five families and the rest looking on. No, no, we'll call a meeting and we'll decide all together what to do. So you keep a good heart, a Mhairi, like your mother.'

After this we all broke out talking, a comfortable talk like people with their minds made up and grandmother made us a meal and it was like a feast we were all so friendly and of the one mind.

7 The Sheriff Officer

We boys were in a state of high excitement after that. We staged many a mock battle, leaping out on sheriff officers from behind boulders and chasing them with blood curdling screams, snatching 'papers' and making off into the hills with them. Whatever happened the five men were not to put a finger on the eviction notices. Archie told us that the crofters were going to post us on all the hill tops overlooking the road and we were to give warning if strangers were seen coming.

I'm telling you we were longing for that fortnight to pass and it seemed to take twice as long as usual but at last the day came and we were told to take up our position on the hill which overlooked the schoolhouse.

'You'll keep your eyes on Clach-a' Bhottail and when you see the boys there wave a flag you'll come straight to the beach at Balmeanach,' said Ian.

I said we could see the hill away beyond that again. 'You can see the hill no doubt but you'd not see a flag.'

Well, we sat there feeling very important with the whole safety of the five on our shoulders and we never took our eyes off the road but as the day passed and nothing happened we began to weary and to think out ways of passing the time. Hughie and I took to wrestling. It wasn't a very good place for it. We lost our footing and rolled downhill and quarrelled at the bottom each blaming the other till we heard a shout and looking up in alarm we saw Ian looking as black as a thunder cloud.

'Is this how you keep watch?' he demanded when we had panted back up. 'Are you wanting grandfather to be turned out?'

'I am not!'

'And how would you see a flag waving and you rolling downhill like a couple of barrels?'

We felt very small. Ian threatened to send us both home but in the end he divided us telling Donald and Hugh to come first thing in the morning and Archie and me to stay where we were till it grew dark.

Archie and I settled down but we agreed between us that it was better for one to watch the road and for the other to rest his eyes for in the bright spring sunshine it was hard to be staring at the white road all the time.

I was having a rest when the school skailed. The big scholars took the road at a run.

'Just what we used to do,' Archie murmured.

'We were faster!' Of course we were. The little ones came trailing along and stopped at the top to stare up at us.

'Hurry up!' I shouted, 'or the sheriff officer will get you.'

You should have seen them take to their heels as if the township bull had been after them. They were in such a panic they kept falling.

'You shouldn't have done that!' Archie protested. Well, I never thought they'd believe me. I suppose they pictured a sheriff officer as a sort of water kelpie. I whistled a tune and shrugged off Archie's reproaches. It was dusk before Ian came to release us and we were very hungry.

The following day was just as fine with the north wind blowing and the sky like a great blue bowl over us, the white horses coming charging down from the far north. I was lying on my side digging out pig nut with my fingers to have something to chew when Archie gripped my arm and pointed. They were waving a flag on Clach-a' Bhotaill. The sheriff officer was coming!

Well, we had it all worked out so we parted, Archie to go up and warn all the Gedintailor tenants and me to run to the Balmeanach beach.

I went downhill at breakneck speed and then at a jog
trot on the flat part of the road. Once off it again I put
on speed and shouted as I passed each house 'The Sheriff
Officer! the Sheriff Officer!' Women and children came to
the door but I kept on for the beach where the men were.
When I reached the edge of the green bank above the
shore I cupped my hands to my mouth and gave a halloo. I
had to do it three times before they heard but when they
did they came running, their sickles in their hands.

They came streaming up the bank, the women keeping
up with the men. I joined grandfather and together we
hurried to gain the road.

'Put down your sickles!' he ordered. They made a pile of
them and then we all hastened to put as much space as
possible between the dreaded sheriff officer and the homes of
the wanted men.

When we came to the burn we saw the Gedintailor men
waiting and farther off three men walking towards us. We
were just in time.

I was at the back of the crowd and I couldn't see a thing
so I wriggled clear and climbed up on the bank above the
road. I found Archie and Donald and stayed beside them.

'Why are there three?' I asked.

'The sheriff officer and the ground officer—I don't know
the other one.'

Well, of course I knew the ground officer already and my
arm kept a remembrance of the way his fingers had dug into
it. I was curious to see the sheriff officer. To my surprise
he had quite a pleasant, open face and otherwise there was
nothing remarkable about him.

The crowd blocked the road so the three men halted and
Angus Martin the sheriff officer addressed them in a cheerful,
friendly kind of way saying, 'Well, fheara, and how are
things with you?'

I suppose no one was expecting this and no one knew

how to reply. Martin looked from one to the other and his eyebrows went up but then grandfather said, 'We are well. I trust you are in good health!'

'Good life!' I whispered to Archie but he shushed me.

Martin smiled, 'I'm middling, thank you. We are having a fine spell of weather for the time of year.'

'That is so,' agreed grandfather.

There was a silence and then Martin giving a little cough said, 'Well, friends, with your leave I must be about my business. Will you be so good as to let me past?'

The crowd moved closer together.

'What is your errand?' asked Neil, Archie's father.

'I have papers to deliver.' There came a low, menacing sound from the people on the road.

'Give us the papers!'

But Martin shook his head. 'Now, now, you know I can't do that. I have my duty to carry out—'

'Duty!' cried Mor Chaluim, a great block of a woman, and she went up close to Martin and he fell back a step. 'Duty! a nasty, dirty duty you have too turning on your own kinsmen! Was there no other way open to you to keep body and soul together but by being running dog to the factor?'

My grandmother advanced on the young man, 'What brought you here, Ewen Robertson? Is it turning sheriff officer you are too and your beard not grown?' This sally got a loud laugh. Grandmother looked round saying, 'Would you believe it! His grandfather was a decent man!' and then she swung back to face Robertson. 'He'd be ashamed to see the company *you* keep. Be off home with you and think twice before you join the likes of these.' And she cast a scornful glance at the other two.

Ewen didn't know where to look but Martin cried, 'Now, now, we're wasting time. I have papers to deliver. I see some of you are here so I can hand them over.'

At this the crowd surged forward and someone shouted

'Give us the papers!'

I think Martin was beginning to understand he'd not get through but he tried, I'll say that for him.

'Come! Come! you're not doing yourselves any good getting on the wrong side of the Law!'

'Being on the right side of the Law hasn't done us much good either!' retorted Neil and everyone burst out laughing. I had my eyes fixed on Martin's face and I could see him hesitate. There was a sudden lull and with the end of human voices I could hear the gulls calling as they quartered the freshly ploughed fields.

Martin's hand went to his inside pocket and he took out the hated papers.

'Burn them! Burn them!' shrieked the women. Donald darted off to his home and came back carrying a burning peat in a tongs. The crowd parted to let him through—and I wished my house had been the nearest—

'Burn away then!' said Angus Martin with a shrug but that would not do either.

'You brought them! You burn them!'

Martin took a look round as if he imagined help might be near but there was only ourselves facing him. He took back the packet and held it to the smouldering peat but the paper was too thick to catch. Only the edges of it charred and blackened.

'Blow on the peat!' commanded Mor and the rest of us applauded. This was our day and we were giving the orders! The sheriff officer blew and blew till the peat glowed red, then he stripped off a small bit of paper. When he had got this to burn he held it to the summonses until the whole bundle went up in flames. Not till the last blackened scrap had blown away did we let out a shout of triumph. The papers were no more. There could be no eviction now!

Martin joined his companions and they faced the way they had come but we were not finished with them yet.

Mor Chaluim rushed forward and emptied a bucket of slops right over the young man. He choked and spluttered clawing the dirt away from his face and started to run. We laughed and laughed as Martin and Beaton went after him. Maybe *they* were thankful there was just the one bucket. I bent down, found a stone and let fly. It caught Beaton on the back and with that he took to his heels and we went whooping after them sending anything we could lay our hands on in their direction, sticks, stones and lumps of earth. We had good aim too I'll say that for us. It was all those nights herding cows, keeping them out of the corn with a well aimed shot. We went up the Cuing in hot pursuit. Once over the top the hunted men could see the schoolhouse and knew they'd be safe if they could reach it.

'Come on!' I yelled to Archie and he and I were at their heels. With the last stone I got Martin on the cheek and the blood spurted out. One for Ben! One for Ben! but we had reached the bridge. The school gate opened and there stood the Master. He stood staring and I saw the hunted men go past him without a word and make for the house. The Master came out on to the road and shook his fist at us and at that we began to cool off. We retreated slowly up the hill sorry the chase was over.

It was long before we could calm down. We raced off to Archie's, leaping on the dyke and brandishing imaginary weapons, rushing right round the house whooping wildly till all the little ones were frightened and the older ones laughing with glee.

But then the men began to gather round Neil seated at the side of the house out of the wind. We stopped our antics to hear what they were saying. There was a great deal of argument about what would happen next but in the end everyone was agreed that if we could keep the papers from being delivered within the next fortnight then the five wanted men would be safe after that from the Law. We were all pleased about that.

But when I reached home it was a different story entirely.

'You will see what will come of this!' Uncle Donald was shouting, his face whiter than ever and his eyes staring. 'Harm will come of it, nothing but harm! You teach the young to defy their elders! You will reap a bitter harvest!'

'They'll do what we tell them!' retorted Ian looking grim.

'You give them leave to throw stones at the officers of the Law! And you think that is good!'

'Do you want your father to be turned out of his house?'

'You will not help him by breaking the Law! He who breaks the Law breaks his own head!'

I knew where Donald got that one! Straight from the Master! They were standing glaring at one another and I had a rare chance of shying a stone at Uncle Donald. My fingers itched but I knew better when Ian was about. He swung round on me now.

'What are you gaping at? Go and clear the stones off the piece I ploughed yesterday.'

Good life! The field was nothing but stones so presently when Ian was out of sight I slipped off and found the others and we relived our victory many times.

But would you believe it! Before that fortnight was over I'd have been pleased to pick the stones off that field. There we were perched up on that hill for hours on end and was I tired of it! Some days it was so wet and misty that if they had come they'd have been on to us before we'd marked them.

We built ourselves a rough shelter with driftwood we hauled up from the beach and we crawled inside when the rain came down heavy but always with one of us keeping a good look-out for we were determined not to be caught off guard a second time. But to say truth even stone gathering or a spell at the tangle on the beach would have seemed like a holiday to that weary watch.

But on the last day we made a fire and cooked a pot of potatoes. Twice the pot tilted over and spilt half its water over the flames and we had to blow them back to life but when at last the potatoes were ready we ate them with great satisfaction.

And when we went home that night everyone praised us and told us we had done well. Grandfather and the rest were safe from the sheriff officer and his eviction notices.

8 *The Battle*

If Effie had not had the toothache—I sometimes think of
that. Well, what difference would it have made? A good
deal, I believe.

But I had better tell how it happened. Mother woke
me telling me to run to the Master's and tell his wife that
Effie was bad with the toothache. Suppose they were still in
bed? Norah would be up—she was not allowed a long lie and
she would tell her mistress.

So I set off and it was not till I left the shelter of the
house that the wind caught me. It pushed me along as if
I had been no heavier than thistle down—and the rain! Its
long slanting lines were near solid. It was sleety and cold and
I guessed it was snow higher up. Except for the cold I would
have enjoyed being blown along but I was wet in no time.
Once over the top I was in shelter and could draw breath
and look out to sea where the spindrift rose in sheets.

Nearing the edge of the next flat the wind caught me
such a buffet I was lifted clean off my feet and landed in a
bog. Not that that mattered much I was so wet already. I
wasn't hurt so I crawled on hands and knees till I could
drop down once more and from there the sheep track ran
in the shelter till I reached the road. Not far to go now. I
was soon at the top of the schoolhouse brae and there!
I could scarce believe my eyes—I saw a crowd coming
marching down the brae opposite, the front of it well past
the birch copse, the rear still among the trees. I crouched,
bewildered. Who were they? What did they want? But
they'd told me grandfather was safe! This did not spell
safety.

I could not reach the schoolhouse now, I remember thinking. Effie's toothache! I could do nothing about that. And then what I must do filled my mind. I must warn grandfather. I must run.

I faced about and head down struggled against the full force of the gale. Try as I might to keep going every now and then a blast brought me to a full stop and I would stand leaning against the wind and then on again when the fury slackened. I was worried sick that it slowed my pace. I don't believe it kept me back all that much but it added to my fears and feeling of helplessness.

Not three men this time but nearer a hundred! How could I save grandfather? There was so little time, so little time. I stubbed my toe on a stone and cried out with the pain and ran on, crouched almost double. No use trying to plan. All I could do was warn them, just warn them. I ran through the dyke and down the bank in leaps. Here I was in the shelter and could raise my head and breathe. I lifted the latch and old Tweed barked loudly. Grandmother was already up and she turned in astonishment to see my dripping figure.

'Sam!' she cried. 'Whatever's wrong?'

'They're coming! They're coming!' I gasped out.

'Who's coming? Is it the sheriff officer? I'll deal with *him*.'

'No—not—it's an army! They've got helmets!'

At that she cried out and ran to the closet shouting to grandfather to jump out of bed for they were on to him.

Calum shouted from the bedroom, 'Where are they Sam?'

'They'll be at the Cuing by now! Oh! hurry, do hurry.'

He came through from the bedroom pulling a jersey over his head, grabbing his boots from under the settle.

'What can we do?' he said. 'There's no time to get people together..'

'You can get to the caves in Aird and hide there till

they're gone,' said grandmother. She was the calmest of
us all.

Uncle Calum nodded. 'Yes, I'll get the other three—'

'And send word up to Peinchorran!' grandmother shouted
after him.

'Did you warn them on the way along, Sam?'

'No I hadn't time. Everyone's in bed—I'd have taken too
long.'

'Well, run to Duncan Dubh's house and tell the boys to
get the Gedintailor men. Warn them—'

But I did not stay. I knew well enough what danger to
avoid. I banged against the door and at last they woke.
Once awake they were quick enough and I watched two of
the boys disappear over the top before I ran back. I was
just at the end of the house when I saw helmeted men in
huge coats at the top of the brae. I shouted a last warning
as I ran past the door then jinked round the corner out of
sight. The next thing was the clatter of their boots on the
cobbles and the bang at the door. For the life of me I had
to poke my head out to see what was happening. I was
just in time to see the first man shoulder his way in. But
if he went in quick he came out quicker with a yell you
might have heard in Raasay and there was grandmother after
him brandishing the three legged pot she had had on the
fire.

'That'll teach you a lesson!' she shouted in Gaelic, 'and
give you a wash too only it wasn't hot enough!'

They did not understand Gaelic but they knew scalding
water when it met their skin. The first man went on scream-
ing and they stood hesitating but not for long.

'Grab the witch!' one shouted. It took two men to hold
her while three pushed into the house. I kicked at them as
hard as I could before the other came out dragging grandfather with them. He suddenly looked small to me but then
the police were great burly men. His jacket was only half
on, his boots were not tied and his hair on end.

'You're the heroes!' jibed grandmother, 'three of you to hold an old man!'

'Hold your tongue! you old besom—' shouted one of them. All I could see of him was a blue chin and a red nose coming out from under the helmet.

They hustled their prisoner up the hill and grandmother and I followed hard at their heels. I saw people coming running from their houses everywhere.

'There's help coming!' Grandmother nodded.

'We'll save him, Sam!' she shouted going up the brae as if she were no more than twenty.

Everyone was making for the road and when we reached it it was to find a crowd of our neighbours surrounding the band of policemen. The women were shouting at the police taunting them with coming in such numbers for five un-armed men. I could hear snatches and then the howling of the wind swept their words out to sea and swept away too the orders of the officers. At least I think it must have done for there was great confusion. Then Mor Chaluim flung the first stone and at once every woman there and all the men began to fling stones and there was a hail of them to add to the wind and rain. The boys joined me and we kept at it flinging every stone we could lay hands on.

There was a wee man strutting about in a great taking, shouting away for all he was worth but we couldn't make out a word he said but seeing he was giving orders we aimed a few stones at him. I got him fair on the back of the head and he spun round, his eyes starting out of their sockets.

'You will suffer for this—all of you! All of you!' But his voice was no more than a thin pipe and the wind blew his words over the Sound and we threw another volley of stones for good measure.

It was a hurly-burly. I was dancing in and out and the other lads with me. We had the sense not to get close for one policeman could have broken our bones with ease but we were too quick for them and then I noticed all of a sudden that a bunch of police were drawing their batons and charging down on the women. I shouted to them to run but either they did not hear or were too angry to think of escape for they stood up to the men and got sore blows because of their courage.

'Sam! Sam!' Hugh was calling to me, 'Look! they're off!' and sure enough the main body was off down the road with grandfather and the rest in the middle of the troop.

Hugh and I chased after them but when we saw that the bulk of the crofters were heading up hill. I was fair puzzled for a moment till I heard a shout of 'The Cuing! The Cuing!' and then I understood. At the Cuing there is just the width of the road between the hill rising steep on the left and the cliffs going down to the shore on the right. Just the width of the road! That was the place to hold the police, yes, if we could reach it in time. Men were coming up behind shouting 'The Cuing! The Cuing!' and others ran ahead. Hugh and I kept company over the burn and through Neil's croft and on over the rough ground till we reached just above the Cuing and found Neil, Ewen and Ian all there. I sank down beside Archie, my breath searing my throat. He grinned at us.

'Get stones, boys!' roared Neil—and my goodness, gale or no gale we heard *him* all right and we darted here and there gathering stones in piles. If we could hold them anywhere this was the place. Donald was at look-out, lying flat. The rest of us were hidden by the curve of the hill.

The worst part of a fight is waiting for it to begin, men marching along the road, us waiting in ambush for the right moment. Surely, surely they must be close now. Was Donald asleep? No, no such thing. He yelled a warning and we got to our feet as the first men swung into sight on the road beneath.

'Now, boys!' shouted Neil and we let fly. The police doubled up and made to run the gauntlet but another volley, rocks as well as stones made them halt. We let out a yell of triumph. The whole police force was down there below us huddling close to the hill to escape our fire. As soon as a head appeared we flung a volley and they jinked back in. But this did not please the little man and he was shouting to them to advance and rush us. We had the advantage though of being above them and a stone is better than a baton when you're out of reach. So it went on and I believe we could have kept them there for hours if the women had not lost all sense of caution. Instead of staying clear up on the hillside they clambered closer and closer shouting insults.

'Come back!' Neil ordered, 'Come back!' but they would not heed till at last the police charged up the hill. Their batons came hard down on the women, but we boys kept clear and I got the one who had hit grandmother, got him right on the nose with a sharp stone and the blood gushed out. I had no time to enjoy my revenge for their cry went up 'They're away!' Sure enough the main body with the prisoners was going like the mischief up the road while the constables were keeping us busy on the hillside.

'After them, boys! After them!' Neil yelled. Off we went at the double but now we had to pick stones up as we ran and this hindered us a little. Still we did damage, getting a man here and another there but all the while they were getting farther and farther from us until at last we boys were alone.

'Sam!' Archie shouted. 'Come back, Sam, it's no use.' I looked behind me and they had all stopped. In front the police were hurrying the prisoners out of my sight.

'Why did you stop?' I said angrily. He shook his head. The water was sluicing off him, his black hair plastered to his head, giving him the look of a seal. He had a cut on his chin and another on his cheek. He was a sight.

'We can't rescue them alone, Sam, just you and me!'

'They shouldn't have stopped! They shouldn't have stopped! We could have saved them!'

'No we couldn't, Sam, not once they were clear of the Cuing. We hadn't a chance after that.'

I could have wept with rage. To let them go! Oh! it was shameful. We dragged our way up the steep brae. With every step I felt more tired. My hand was cut over the knuckles, my knee was painful and now that the fight was over I had time to feel the cold. We were soaked to the skin and the wind as high as ever felt as if it blew clean through us.

It wasn't just tiredness, it was knowing we'd been beaten that took the heart out of us.

At the top of the hill we came on the women weeping and the men standing by.

'They've taken our men,' they complained together, 'no food in their bellies and no coat to their back.'

'My bairns! My poor bairns!' cried Peter's wife. 'Without a father.' Grandmother rocked herself to and fro. 'Alasdair takes a cold that easy!'

Just then the Peinchorran men came running and the women turned angrily upon them.

'Why did you not come in time?'

'We came the minute we got word,' said Angus Stewart. 'Why did you not keep better watch?'

'The time was up! We thought they would not come any more!'

That was the fatal mistake! The women broke out into lamentations. I had never seen grandmother weep before. It took the heart out of me.

I tugged at her sleeve. 'Did Mother go home? Where's Ian?'

She lifted her head and looked at me then.

'Oh! Sam, did you not see? She ran to have a last word with her father and they hit her, hit her on the back of the head—' Grandmother sobbed aloud.

'They carried her home, Ian and Neil and the rest—oh!

my arm—I think it's broken but my heart is worse.'

'Come, come!' cried Angus, 'sitting here is not going to do us any good. Mor! help Alasdair's wife home and the rest of you make for your houses. We can do no more here than die of cold.'

This was true and Archie and I made off up the brae as Angus marshalled the women on to the road. Archie went off to his own home and I carried on in the teeth of the gale.

I remembered—no, it was not remembering so much as seeing a picture inside my head of my father and me coming home one stormy evening and of the wind blowing me over and of how he made me catch hold of his jacket and in that fashion he crawled forward with me clinging on behind. I was only small at the time. And over the years I could hear him laugh and make a joke of the storm till he had me laughing too. Well, he had been drowned not long after. There was no one left to help or praise me.

The squall went by lifting spindrift high out in the bay. I got to my feet for the last stretch. When I drew near the house I could see women about the door. I could hear their wails. The sound made my skin prickle. What good did crying do? They were keening as if someone had died.

I joined the group at the door but such a fear got hold of me that I could not speak. Kate Eoghain saw me and cried out 'Oh! Sam, your mother is lying there without a word out of her since they knocked her down!' and another said 'Not a word out of her! Poor thing! Poor thing! Perhaps she'll never speak again.'

I turned and ran but their voices followed, wailing and lamenting and when I could no longer hear them the wind howled in my ears.

9 *To The Rescue*

I crept up to the fire in Neil's house. I was so cold my fingers were blue. Archie made room for me and we sat drying ourselves while Chrissie swabbed timidly at her father's cuts and he kept protesting 'Is it a bull's hide you think I have that you rub so hard? Your mother should be here to see to me!'

Chrissie got all flustered and spilt some of the hot water on his arm and went red and shouted to Murdina.

'Can you not go and milk the cows? Do you think I can do everything? Have I two pairs of hands?'

'If you had one good pair you'd do,' commented her father dryly. I sat shivering, my teeth clacking and wished they'd stop quarrelling and get us some food. I felt faint for the want of it.

Luckily Neil did too and as soon as he was bandaged to his satisfaction shouted for porridge. Chrissie flung oatmeal into the boiling water and stirred for dear life. In spite of that I never tasted porridge with so many lumps in it.

Neil had leisure now to talk to me.

'Is it yourself, Sam? You'll soon be dry. Turn your back when your front's done. The wife is up with your mother. Now don't you worry! Women! They always make out a person's worse than they are! Och! It's just their way and they mean no harm but if you listen to them they take your heart down. Your mother will soon be all right. Many a one I've seen knocked out by a blow and an hour or two later they would be sitting up and calling for their dinner! Your mother will be making your porridge tomorrow or my name's not Neil Ceannaiche!'

He took such a load off my mind that if he had asked me to jump off a cliff I'd have done it without hesitation. As it was I could now enjoy the bowl of porridge and milk which Chrissie gave me.

It was wonderfully warm and comfortable in there and we steamed in the heat of the fire. With food inside me I felt like a new man.

Archie asked me what had taken me out so early on a wild morning and I told him about Effie's toothache. Well, she'd need to find another messenger now for I could never face the Master after this! He'd have had his eye to the window and seen the fugitives go by.

Presently men began to drift in and at first all the talk was of how we had failed to drive the police off. Everyone was low in his spirits. We had kept watch for so long and given up just when a watch was needed.

They shook their heads and admitted that they could not have been right about the fourteen days. But in a way what did it matter? With an army like that what could we have done anyway?

But Neil denied this. If we had had time to gather everyone and if the Peinchorran men had taken the police in the rear then the five men would never have smelt the inside of a prison! They were big, stalwart fellows, the Glasgow police but what of that and Ewen told us that the captain of the *Glencoe* had refused to sail with them aboard and it had been left to the mate to bring them into Portree the night before. There were good men alive yet, Neil observed and then he began to make up verses praising the efforts of the Braes men and of the women too and that was right for I had seen them with my own eyes attacking the policemen. They'd been grand then. It was only afterwards that they wept and cried but seeing they were women I suppose they couldn't help that.

Well, more and more people came crowding in and Neil made more and more verses. He had the knack and in every verse he praised someone new. One time it was Mor Chaluim and then Kate Lachlainn and then my grandmother and whose turn was it next but me! I had run like the deer on the mountain and had fought like one of the young Feinn! Well, I blushed as red as the fire and felt so pleased I could have dashed out of the house and started fighting all over again, my pains and aches forgotten.

Well, the upshot was we decided to march on Portree. When we reached it we'd get a ship's mast down in Sligneach where the boats were beached and with it we'd batter down the jail door and no one would dare to stop us!

In the late afternoon we set off. The rain had stopped and the wind fallen to a breeze. The clouds were breaking up looking like the ragged fleeces of poor sheep. Water was everywhere, gurgling in the ditches by the road, coming swirling down the hillside turning burns into foaming torrents. The air was fresh and clean and I felt as I marched at Archie's side that it was just the day for heroic action.

But presently I found the pace too slow. Neil's praises were in my head 'fleet as a deer' and I resolved to be just that. I'd go ahead and act as scout for the main party coming behind.

I was soon jog trotting along the main road with a bare two miles between me and the village. A bare two miles between me and grandfather. It's all right, I said to him in my heart, it's all right. We're coming! We won't leave you in prison.

I heard a strange noise ahead of me and stopped short to listen. Round the bend came soldiers, a piper at their head. It was the drone of the pipes I had heard and now the whole troop was swinging down on me. I made one jump off the road and up hill I went like a hunted hare. I flung myself down behind a boulder, the only cover there was. Frightened as I was curiosity got the better of me and I peeped round the rock. Good life! this was worse even than the Glasgow police. These were soldiers armed with rifles!

B.O.B.   F

What with that and the skirl of the pipes my heart fell. How could we fight an army? They looked neither to right nor to left but swung by below and then I saw what I had to do. I must get down to the river and ford it somehow and so get back to fight alongside my friends.

I ran across the wet field back to the river but I knew at once that I could not ford it. It was in spate and I would have been carried down it like a cork if I had ventured into it. Put out by this delay I ran along the bank making for the footbridge. When I was nearly at it I saw to my astonishment that the soldiers had passed the Braes road and were making for Glenvarrigill farm house. I looked up and saw the Braes men at the top of the hill. The sun held them in its last rays and that was right for to me they were heroes.

I started running the last hundred yards to the footbridge, expecting to meet them there. But there was no one. I looked up the road and down. Not a soul in sight and the soldiers themselves had disappeared. I could not understand what had happened. I began running up the hill hoping against hope to meet them coming down but when I reached the top and saw the empty moorland stretching ahead I knew that the Braes men had lost heart and turned for home. I sat down and tears trickled down my face. I flung myself down on the wet grass and sobbed my heart out. There was no one to see me. When at last I sat up it was sunset. The sky in the west glowed crimson and all the little clouds were pink but far in the east the pink faded to grey.

It was clear that if I was to do something I must get under way. What could I do alone, I asked myself and shook my head in answer. I didn't know. I had no plan, but one thing I was sure of I was not going home, my tail between my legs.

It was twilight when I stood in the Square and faced the jail. It was a solid stone building and I saw at once that all my hopes of breaking in were so much moonshine. I had often climbed rock faces after sheep but on these there had always been at least a toe hold. Here was nothing but smooth stone and no window within reach. But the door! That was different altogether. If only the Braes men had come we could have battered it to bits and let the prisoners free.

Well! that was it. I could not stand all night in the Square. What was I to do now? I knew I could not walk the seven miles home. I was so tired I could scarce stand upright. My father's sister however lived in Sluggans, a bare half-mile out of the village on the far side. She'd give me a bite and a corner to lie in. Yes, that was the sensible thing to do. I swallowed the ache in my throat, took one long last look at the prison and—a sound made me turn about sharply but too late. A policeman had me by the jacket.

'What you doing here?' he asked in a slurred voice. 'What you up to? You got friends in there? Eh? Is that it? Well, have you lost your tongue? Can't speak the Queen's English! Heathen, just heathen, that's what you all are up here.'

As you can guess I wasn't standing still listening to all this. I was struggling like a wild cat. I'd have done better to stay quiet for all I got was a blow on the side of the head that left me dizzy. I hung limp and he had a good look at me and gave a grunt.

'Thought as much, thought as much, seen you before, red-headed rascal, throwing stones, got my mate on the nose, you did, a decent chap, George, and father of five. Well, that's right, so it is, it's right you should be here and right for me to—'

He stopped and struggled with his thoughts. He was considering in what way he could punish me for what I had done to George (that must have been the chap with the blue chin).

I was sweating with fear and any desire I may have had earlier in the day to be known as a good marksman seeped right out of me. My legs felt like jelly. A quick blow I could stand. I'd had many a one in my day but to have to hang there listening to him trying to make up his mind how best to hurt me made my heart race and the blood beat in my ears. I gave a desperate jerk and struck out with my bare feet at his legs but bare feet are not much use against legs like his. He stumbled, it's true, but then he let fly at me with his boot catching the calf of my leg and I howled with pain for the tackets tore my flesh.

'Shut up, will you, you hooligan!' he roared, 'I'll give you in charge so I will. No, I won't, I'll get you into a quiet corner and make a pulp of your face. Your own mother won't know you!'

I was desperate and shouted as loud as I could for help. They would put me in prison, no doubt, but I'd be safer there than with this terrible man. He caught me another buffet on the side of my head. In spite of the pain I yelled once more and to my joy heard voices and footsteps coming at a run.

'What are you doing, Constable?'

'Taking this young perisher in charge, sir.'

'You are not on duty here, I think. Are you not one of the Glasgow police?'

'Yes, sir, that's right, sir, but I found this young hoodlum in suspicious circumstances—'

'You were striking him!' the voice was very cold now. 'Mr Kemp, take this man's number and I shall go straight to the Police Station and lay a complaint against him.'

'Don't leave me!' I managed to whisper but I didn't need to. The policeman let go of me and I slipped like an empty sack on to the pavement.

When I came to I found myself being held up by two strangers, one on each side of me. My legs didn't seem to belong to me and I would have fallen at every step if they had not held me up.

'You're all right, now,' the first voice said, 'we'll look after you. Just try to walk. We haven't far to go!'

Thus encouraged I did my best but it wasn't very good. They got me to the steps which I knew led down to the harbour. We started slowly down them and then I smelt the sea coming up and a smell of rotten fish and I retched and spewed, not that I had anything in my stomach to be sick on but just bile.

'Poor lad!' said the other man, 'you're in a bad way. But it's all right, the wife will look after you. Almost there now!'

So going slowly and carefully they got me down the steps and along the street and then they turned in at a door. It was too narrow for three of us abreast so one man supported me while the other went up and opened a door. I saw a ring of surprised-looking faces and then I fainted.

I had never done such a thing before and when I came to myself I was bewildered and did not know where I was. I was lying on a bench and a woman was washing my sore leg. I lay thinking I was lucky not to have Chrissie bathing my cuts. This woman was very gentle and even at that she hurt me a lot. I could hear talking going on around and sometimes it was near me and sometimes far away and I wondered muzzily where they went to when I could hardly hear them. But very soon after that the room steadied and the voices stayed in the one place. I tried to sit up.

'Oh! are you better now? Well, that's good. Now don't move. I'll bandage your cuts.' The woman had a pleasant open face and a soft voice and I did what she told me.

In the glimpse I had of it I could see the room was full of people, men mostly. They were saying it was a shame for a policeman to be attacking a mere boy. What could a boy do anyway? I thought I could tell them different but I was afraid to say anything and then I saw a fair-headed man looking down on me. He had blue eyes in a fresh-coloured face but he was frowning.

'I've seen you somewhere before!' he said. I was so

scared by this that I thought the best thing I could do would be to get away quick and I did manage to put my feet on the floor before they stopped me.

'Now then, Mr Ramsay,' said the woman, 'you're upsetting the lad. Let him rest a wee while and then he'll tell you where he was.'

But Mr Ramsay was smiling. 'I've got it!' he exclaimed. 'It's William Tell himself!'

Now I was convinced I'd been right to be afraid. I took a quick look round and there on the dresser stood an oil lamp just like the Master's. Now I knew they would think it wrong to throw stones at sheriff officers and policemen.

Was the boy in the battle, they asked Mr Ramsay, in the battle up in Braes? And he nodded. 'That red head of his I'd know it anywhere.' I'd often wanted to be black but never more than at that moment. Since this man had been in the battle he'd been with the police!

They all plied me with questions, was I from Braes? Was I alone? Was it true the Braes men were going to release the prisoners? But I would not answer.

'Leave the boy alone,' Mrs Kemp said. (I was in Alec Kemp's house, and he was a tailor, I learnt afterwards.) 'Can you not see he's white as a sheet. Are you hungry?'

I tried to make out whether I was hungry or not. No, I was still squeamish although I had eaten nothing since Chrissie's porridge but I was not hungry. I was thirsty. Mrs Kemp made tea for me and promised me a proper meal later on.

They left me alone for a little while and I sipped the hot tea. Mr Ramsay was talking away to the others and from what he was saying I began to think he must be on our side but why then was he with the police?

So when he got round to questioning me again I asked him straight. He seemed quite taken aback for a moment gazing at me with his eyes wide. 'Why, he thinks I was one of Sheriff Ivory's merry men!' And he put back his head and laughed heartily.

'It was a natural enough mistake seeing you were with them,' said a tall man with a dark beard, Roderick Macmillan he was, and had a shop.

'You're right!' said Mr Ramsay, 'I'll explain, boy. I'm a reporter, that's a man who writes for the papers, the man who sends news to the daily paper and that's what I was doing up in Braes in that storm this morning! And when I got back to Portree at the tail of the the procession the first thing I did was to pop into the Post Office and send off the whole story. I was drenched to the skin, the water was pouring off my clothes on to the floor and outside they were booing Sheriff Ivory and all the high officials who tagged along behind him. Do you know,' he added looking at the company, 'it's an awesome sound, the booing of a crowd and it takes a brave man to stand up to it, a braver man than Sheriff Ivory! He made for the Royal Hotel as fast as a rabbit for its burrow, and to be frank I don't blame him for that. The Post Office was my rabbit burrow.'

But they did not believe him. 'We weren't booing you, Charles, it was the Sheriff and the other high-ups. I think the whole village was there lining the road from the school to the Square! And a pretty bedraggled lot the fiscals and lawyers looked!'

This was music to my ears. I had had no notion that the Portree people would support us. I wanted to hear more and especially about sending the story away to the papers.

Charles Ramsay came back to that of his own accord (I was too shy to ask). 'It will be in every paper in Scotland tomorrow morning. And we'll have the whole of Scotland laughing at a sheriff-principal being chased by a few crofters with stones!'

I was puzzled by all this talk of a sheriff-principal and Sheriff Ivory. 'I didn't see the sheriff,' I managed to say, for to my mind a sheriff-principal would cut a very grand figure indeed.

'Not see him? A wee man strutting up and down and piping out orders to the police inspectors?'

'Oh! *him*,' I said enlightened. 'I hit him with a stone.'

The whole company roared with laughter and my spirits began to revive.

'He's in a terrible temper,' Mrs Kemp said placidly. 'I heard from my cousin who's a waitress in the hotel. He wouldn't stay in bed but jumped out to begin a long letter, goodness knows who he was writing to and Lachie Ross is running about saying his hotel is ruined—no one will come any more when they hear what happened to the sheriff!'

Nobody took this much to heart and it was then Mr Ramsay began asking me questions. I had to begin at the very beginning, with Effie's toothache, that is, and follow the story right through. There was only one bit I didn't like to tell of, when the crofters went home but no one there did more than smile a bit.

'The soldiers!' said Alec Kemp. 'Oh! that was only Lachie Ross and the Volunteers! and he'd run if he saw a crofter anywhere near him though he wouldn't have arms at all.'

'We had stones,' I said. I wasn't too fond of this bit about unarmed crofters. They laughed again and said I was a hero (which I knew very well I wasn't but I liked hearing it all the same) and Mr Macmillan said I was quite right for had not David defeated Goliath with stones from the brook.

They were talking among themselves after that and Mrs Kemp brought me two boiled eggs and scones and butter and I was suddenly ravenous and ate everything but I kept my ears wide open for I did not want to lose a word of what they were saying.

'Maybe it's just as well they turned back, they'd never have got them out of the jail!'

Charles Ramsay nodded thoughtfully. 'Not unless the attack were a complete surprise but I don't think it matters. I wanted some resistance and I got all I hoped for, the police using their cudgels on women whose only crime was to try and defend their husbands and sons. Yes, it's strange, isn't it? I battled my way up this morning (after your cousin had told me what the sheriff was planning) and all the way I was saying to myself if only they'll fight! You see without a fight I'd never get my story into the front page. There would only be a paragraph tucked away somewhere and no one would know. But now we can rouse every radical in the country! Landlords allowing factors to evict tenants at the end of the nineteenth century! No, that is too much for Liberals to stomach. If only the crofters had resisted earlier! But they let themselves be driven out of their land like sheep!'

The others nodded sombrely. That was indeed what had happened, they said. Strong men had stood by and seen their belongings thrown out of their cottages and their wives and children without shelter from the storms of winter.

Ramsay was standing, his arm on the mantelpiece as he talked and listened. He smiled down on me and said, 'The crofters of Braes have changed all that and now we can expose what the landlords have been doing for the last hundred years. In the full blaze of publicity they'll do it no more!'

They went on talking till late and I learnt more history in that room than I'd ever learnt from the Master. At last the party broke up.

'Keep a good heart, Sam,' were Ramsay's last words to me. 'You're not alone in your struggle. We'll be all with you and your grandfather and uncle won't be long in prison and a fig to Ivory! You'll get Ben Lee back yet!'

10 *Home Again*

I limped home next day. I had slept late and I was thinking Ian would have something to say to me when I reached it. I wasn't best pleased then when a window in the school-house was thrown up and the Master's wife called me in. It was the last thing I wanted to do but I did not like to disobey so I walked reluctantly in at the gate and up the stairs.

'Now isn't that lucky Norah saw you coming!' said the Master's wife, 'because I've got a few things here for your mother.' She rummaged in the basket beside her on the table till she found a small bottle. This she told me was a lotion which would cure any wound but only a very little must be used at a time. Then she produced another bottle and told me Mother was to take only a teaspoonful of it night and morning. It was powerful and she must not take more.

I promised to remember the instructions and indeed I was grateful to her for if Mother was fit to take medicine then she must be on the way to recovery. No doubt she had come round all of a sudden as Neil had said she would. I was now in a hurry to be off but the Master's wife stood peering into the basket and I could not leave till she gave it to me.

'Oh! Sam, Sam, this is a sad business! Your grandmother's arm is bad and your own mother lying hurt. See now what happens when you break the Law!'

All the talk I had heard the night before came crowding into my mind and I was just wondering where to start when she ran on, 'I've put in some white scones for your mother for I know she fancies them and I've wrapped up a little bit of fresh butter to tempt her appetite. Now is there

anything else I could give her? Oh! yes, the rhubarb jam.
Look, Norah, in the cupboard. I'm sure there's a few left yet
but even if it was the only one I'd give it to your mother for
she was a nice, kind woman.'

While Norah was fetching the jam I had time to remember the sticks of rhubarb I had stolen out of the garden.
I felt a little uncomfortable.

The Master's wife saw me off saying, 'Be sure and bring
back the basket and the bottles when they're empty.'

I promised I would and thanked her before hurrying off
with the precious basket. White scones and butter! There
was some point in being a schoolmaster when you could
afford such luxuries. How pleased Mother would be and
I could see myself sitting telling her all my adventures.
She would listen to every word and then tell me how brave
I had been to try and rescue grandfather all by myself.

I ran indoors crying 'Mother! Mother! I've got good
things for you. Just see what I've got in the basket!'

But there was no answer. She was lying in the bed and I
went closer and whispered, 'Mother!' but she did not stir.
I was suddenly afraid. Her arm lay outside the coverlet. I
put my hand on it. It was warm. Oh! then it was all right,
she was only sleeping. When she woke and ate the good
things I had brought her she would be fine.

Donald opened the closet door and stood there looking
at me.

'Where have you been?' he demanded, 'was this a time to
disappear when your mother was ill?'

'She's—she's better,' I said lamely.

'No! she's not better. She has not spoken nor eaten since
that terrible fight! See now what happens! Where have
you been?'

'I was—I was with Aunt Bella—' I stammered. Well, I'd
meant to go there and would have gone except for the
policeman.

Donald was opening his mouth to rebuke me, I felt sure, so

I ran out saying I was going to look for Ian.

I hadn't gone far when I met him coming.

'Sam!' he exclaimed, 'where have you been all this time? I've been fair worried and there was enough to worry me without that!'

So then I hurried to tell him my story, all of it and he listened in silence. I took the bandage off my leg to show him the marks of the policeman's boot and he exclaimed, 'Oh! Sam, you were daft going on by yourself!'

'No, but wait till you hear what happened then. It was worth it!' And I told him as much as I could remember and as I have a good memory that was nearly everything. He listened to me as if I had been a man and kept asking about the reporter and what he had said. Would it indeed be in all the papers and would that help us?

Yes, he knew that Alec Kemp and Roderick Macmillan were friends to the crofters and many of the other Portree merchants too but what could they do?

'They booed the sheriff anyway!'

'They took grandfather and the rest away to Inverness prison,' he said. 'No one tried to stop them.' So I told him what Ramsay had said. Then I asked why the crofters had turned back, not that I minded now but I was curious.

'They were expecting the Glen Mor men to join them and then they saw the Volunteers and that took the courage from them.'

'I'm sure Neil was all for going on!'

'Neil!' he chuckled. 'Neil was the keenest of all to go home and I'm certain he made the best time on the road back!'

Well! to think of that. Why Neil had been a hero in the morning. How was it that he could act so cowardly the very same evening?

Late that same evening we went down to his house to hear the news. Neil had just come back from Portree and was full of it. He had a couple of newspapers and as soon as

he saw us exclaimed in wonder, 'Is it not all here, lads!
The whole battle and the welcome we gave the Glasgow
police with their Inspector Donald. It's a welcome they'll
not forget in a hurry.'

Well, I wasn't so impressed by his talk as I would have
been only the day before but I wanted to hear the story out
of the paper. Neil read it aloud and good life! it was all there,
from my grandmother scalding the first policeman to the
time when we brought them to a halt at the Cuing. He
described the place, the sea coming curling in over the rocks
below, and the shrieks of the gale drowning the shrieks of
the women.

We listened in dead silence, hardly able to credit that
what *we* had done was all in the newspaper.

'And do you know this?' Neil said when he had finished,
'every paper that came—and he had ordered double his usual
number—every paper was bought in next to no time and
many had to go away without.'

I hugged my knees and kept to myself the fact that I had
met the reporter. I'm not often so modest but I think I felt
that there was something magical about him and where
there is magic you must keep it secret or it will vanish
away.

Neil had picked up the other paper and now he read a
paragraph out solemnly:— 'When women are so lost to
all sense of modesty and dignity of their sex, when they
not only assail the servants of the Crown as they did
yesterday with oaths and imprecations but actually perform
the part of Amazons and engage them in fierce conflict it
is not remarkable that the objects of their attack should
fail to discriminate too nicely when endeavouring to secure
the prisoners from rescue.'

'Sakes' alive,' cried his wife, 'what does all that mean? It
makes my head go round just listening.'

'Och! you weren't long enough at the school. What's
worrying you? Fail to discriminate? That just means the

police hit out at anyone within reach!'

'And so they did!' cried Kate Lachlainn, 'and when a man's in trouble he'd rather have his wife fighting by him than sitting minding her modesty!'

'Och! well, *The Glasgow Herald*'s a Tory paper,' observed Neil, broadmindedly, 'and it has to stick up for its friends, the landlords.'

We sat thrashing the matter out till late. When I climbed up the hill home the moon was shining above Glamaig, its top white with the snow of yesterday's storm. The air was fresh and sweet scented, a smell of growth, and I heard the snipe drumming as it does on spring evenings. I felt then as if Charles Ramsay was stretching out a hand saying, 'Keep your heart up, Sam! Help's coming. You're not alone any more.'

It was the busiest time of the year now with the ploughing and sowing all to be done and the few sheep we had would be lambing soon. The women had to work in the fields with their men and we did not know how we were to look after Mother.

Ian told me not to go far from the house that next morning.

My first thought when I had the house to myself was to give Mother the medicine but it was no use. It just trickled down her chin. If she could not take medicine and could not eat she would die! A feeling of helplessness came over me and for a few minutes I was close to agreeing with Donald that we had brought this down on our own heads. The excitement of the last two days was over. We were back at ordinary living, only for us it was not ordinary at all without Mother bustling cheerfully about her work as she had always done.

I went out into the sunshine and spent a bad time trying to straighten things out. Then I saw Archie coming with

Floss at his heel and the puppy gambolling about. I was pleased to see him. His mother had sent him up to ask for mine. There was nothing he could say to hearten me but just seeing him did me good. When he was going he said Hugh was on at him about the bitch and if I really didn't want her he'd have to give her away. I sat there looking at her deciding that she was quite the plainest bitch I had ever seen. She was thin too, but no wonder for with eight children to feed there wasn't much left for the animals. I pondered—would she look better when her ribs didn't stick out of her skin. I shook my head. The truth was I didn't mind her being ugly for that way she didn't put me in mind of Ben.

'Oh! all right then, I'll give her to Hugh,' said Archie mistaking my action.

'No, no, I'll have her. I must have a dog and the sooner I start training her the better. Do you think she'll be any good though?'

'Oh! she's got it in her,' he said earnestly, 'she'll make you a good dog yet, Sam, you'll see.'

So we talked about it back and forth till we heard his father bawling for him down below and he had to go. I caught hold of the bitch to keep her from following him. She whined and struggled when I picked her up and carried her into the house. I gave her a bit of oatcake and petted her so that she would take to me and forget about Archie.

Just then the door opened and she nearly got away on me. Who was this but Effie and that striped brute of a tom cat at her heels. The bitch disappeared under the settle the minute Tomas arched his back and spat. It was clear she had no fighting spirit, not like Ben who had chased Tomas up the rowan tree as often as he saw him and that was just the job. If ever I saw a cat that needed putting in its place it was Effie's.

'I've just got a new dog,' I said to her, 'so leave the cat at home when you come over.'

'Is that the welcome you give me,' says she, quite composed, 'and me here to look after your poor mother!'

She did not pay me any more attention but went over to the bed and began talking to Mother just as if Mother could hear her. I didn't like listening and I went out dragging the dog with me. I'd have to get her a name. There were plenty of good names for dogs but a bitch was another matter.

I joined Ian and gave a hand guiding the horses and taking stones out of the path of the coulter. Neil was always complaining of the quantity of stones on his croft but I do believe ours was worse, nothing but stones once you broke the skin of the turf.

I told Ian about Effie when he stopped the horses for a breather at the end of the furrow.

'Is she meaning to stay, Sam?' Ian asked.

'She said she was but oh! Ian don't let her. Get someone else.'

'It's not so easy, Sam. The neighbours come in when they can but they're all busy now with the spring work and Mother ought to have someone all the time. Maybe it will be easier to get someone later on.'

I had to be satisfied with that. When we went home at dinner time Effie had a meal ready for us. But what a meal it was! She had cooked the salt herring to fragments and the potatoes had a bone in their throat. It was hunger alone that forced me to finish the mess on my plate. I kept thinking how good the same meal tasted when Mother cooked it.

When Effie shuffled outside to empty the old tea leaves out of the pot, Ian whispered, 'No wonder her sons went off to Canada and never came back! I'd soon do the same!' I had to giggle and Effie shot me a suspicious look. But when the tea was drawn she went to the cupboard and took out the scones and the fresh butter I had brought home for Mother.

I jumped up saying, 'Those are Mother's. *You* mustn't eat them! They're not for you!'

'Your poor mother can't eat them,' replied Effie taking a

scone in her skinny claw-like hand.

I turned to Ian. 'Don't let her eat them, Ian! I got them for Mother not for her!'

But Ian was no help. 'Wheest, Sam, Mother can't eat them just now. They'll just go hard.'

I sat down but with a choking feeling. I'd had such high hopes for the gifts I'd carried home and now the only person enjoying them was Effie! I took one, split it and put butter on it but before I'd even had a bite she brought out the pot of rhubarb jam and that was too much.

'The jam will keep!' I shouted. 'The jam will keep till Mother—Put it back! Put it back!'

But she paid no more attention to me than to the wind outside and took the paper cover off and stuck her knife into it. But I wasn't having this. I stretched across and grabbed hold of the jar but she had a good grip and so we pulled, one on each side. Ian was saying, 'Oh! stop it, Sam, stop it.' But I wasn't going to stop it. Then she let go suddenly and I fell and the jar slipped to the floor and broke and the jam slowly spread all over.

'Your Mother won't see much of that jam!' cried Effie. I could have struck her with the rage I was in but Ian caught my arm. 'Get outside!' he said in a sudden rage himself. 'Get outside! That's enough of you for one day!' He shoved me out. I was beside myself.

'You don't care! You don't care! You just let her do what she likes!'

He gave me a hard look and slammed the door.

11 *The Doctor*

Ian and I went to see grandmother and found her crouched over the fire and who was with her but Jean, Angus's daughter. She was busy combing grandmother's hair but stopped when we went in.

'What are you stopping for?' grandmother asked her gruffly, 'are you tired already?'

'It's Ian and Sam,' Jean said. 'They've come to see you.'

'It's not before time,' she replied crossly. 'Where have you been that I haven't had a sight of you?'

Ian explained how he had been hurrying on with the ploughing so as to come and plough her croft. She shook her head mournfully.

'It's me that would need help, alone here, not a man near, Calum and Peter and Seumas and Donald all gone. We're poor creatures here without our men.'

She was a changed person no longer full of jokes and beaming kindness, but so down in her spirits that I felt worse now than when I had come in at the door. There was no word of making us tea or even putting butter on a bannock and my inside was clean empty for I could hardly eat the stuff Effie put before us.

Ian and I sat down in silence not knowing what to say. Jean went on combing grandmother's hair and then pinned it up for her.

'You have two pairs of hands here, grandmother,' Ian told her, 'and we'll do all the spring work for you.'

At that she gave something like her old smile and said, 'Oh! Ian, a luaidh, am I not an ungrateful old woman but it is missing Alasdair I am. I'm lying awake all night thinking

of him in that cold prison instead of warm at my side and
not even his good clothes with him! And my arm is that
sore!'

Ian told her he was hearing grandfather and the others
would be out soon. The burghers in Inverness were going to
stand bail for them and they'd get home even if they had
to go back to stand trial later on. I believe he would have
done better to leave out that bit for it frightened her.

'What will they do to them, Ian?' Ian was stuck for an
answer but Jean broke in saying we would all have some tea
and then we'd feel better. There was nothing so bad as an
empty stomach for making a person feel low. Ian began
protesting that we wouldn't wait, we didn't want to be a
cause of more work. She got quite cross at this.

'What do you think I am? Would I let Sam go home
hungry? As if I minded a little work when I have my health
and strength!'

I thought she did not need to be so short with him as I sat
watching her bustling around and wished she lived near us
and could look after Mother. Sure enough I did feel lots better
when I had had enough to eat.

Jean came out with us when we were leaving and her
cheerfulness vanished. 'I'm worried about her, Ian, she's not
sleeping or eating. Is there no way we could get help?'

'We can't afford a doctor.'

'No, but it's a doctor she needs.'

So the little comfort she had given me indoors fell away
from me outside. Grandmother needed a doctor and Mother
needed one even more but we had no money.

The next day was Sunday and I was sitting dangling my
legs over the edge of the crags above Neil's house. I had the
bitch with me on a rope. She wasn't used to me yet and was
still wanting to go back.

I was keeping an eye open for Archie but then I heard the
clip-clop of a horse's hoofs. I sat up at that for it was most
unusual to see anything stirring on a Sunday. I could not

see the road directly below, not till it passed the burn and climbed the hill. I kept my eye on that stretch and saw the pony and trap when they came in sight. I was full of curiosity and off I set to find out what stranger was visiting us and I had a sudden hope that it might be Charles Ramsay come back. But of course it was not. When I caught up I found the Balmeanach boys holding the pony's head and the trap empty.

'It's the doctor!' they told me at once, 'and we're to look after the pony till he comes back but we mustn't give it grass!'

The doctor! Why that was just what Jean had wanted. Had they sent for him? But no one there knew, only that he had come and was going to visit all the people who had been hurt.

He must come and visit Mother then! I didn't care whether we could pay him or not. Perhaps he would let me work for him? Perhaps they would put us to prison for getting doctors when we could not pay but by that time he might have cured Mother and then doing a spell in prison would not matter.

All these thoughts were whirling round in my mind while I waited. The boys were chattering away as usual but I did not take in a word they were saying for the trouble in my mind.

At last we heard people coming and they were all laughing! I could hardly believe it. When people were ill it wasn't right to laugh!

The doctor was a short, thick-set man with a dark beard. He must have been telling a joke for the men laughed again and I had a feeling of being all alone.

'Well! you scamps, have you looked after Ginger properly? Tell the truth now, were you feeding him grass?' He looked at Hugh very threateningly and Hugh looked scared till the doctor chuckled and told him to turn the pony's head homewards. He had mended all the broken heads and arms he was going to mend that day. So he was going away! I stood gawping, my mouth dry. The doctor was putting a foot on the step.

Hugh pulled at my arm. 'Go on, Sam, ask him.'

I stepped forward. 'Please, Doctor—' but he was saying 'You Braes people have strong heads!' and didn't hear me.

'Strong heads and strong arms, Dr Ross, and if ever you need them they're at your service.'

'When I'm on the wrong side of the law I'll remember,' promised the doctor and swung up into the gig.

'Doctor!' I fair shouted the name this time and he heard me.

'What's the matter now? Another patient? You look well enough!'

The men told him about my mother and at that he climbed down from the gig.

'Is it far, boy?' I pointed up the hill. They told him the boys could lead the pony along the road and wait for him above the schoolhouse.

'Is that the best way? Very well, but mind now, no nonsense, you scoundrels or I'll have you horse-whipped!' But the way he said it we knew he did not mean it and the boys just grinned.

I set off up hill at a great pace, I was so pleased to be taking him to see Mother but when I looked back he was far behind and I had to wait.

'Take your time, boy,' panted the doctor as he came up with me. 'It's not chasing deer we are. Tell me now what is your mother complaining of?'

I shook my head. 'She's not complaining at all. She doesn't eat and she doesn't speak!'

'Dear me! Unconscious is she? Since the fight? Was she doing a bit herself?'

'No, she was wanting a last word with my grandfather, Alasdair Bàn, and they hit her on the head.'

'On the back of the head?'

'Yes.'

'Well! well! we'll have to see what we can do!' Dr Ross said briskly and we set off once more.

Ian was outside and looked surprised to see me with the doctor. 'Take me in,' the doctor said after they had exchanged greetings. They went inside and the next thing was that all the women who had been up to see Mother came streaming out.

'Too many people in here!' I heard him declare roundly, ' and this room is far too hot. Open a window!'

Open a window! But we never opened windows. Fresh air was a thing one kept outside. But this did not suit the doctor. When he found that he could not open it he banged the thick glass with his elbow. As he wore a thick great-coat there was no fear of him cutting himself.

'You'll kill her, man,' I could hear him roaring at Ian. 'You'll kill her from the lack of air. You'll finish with your big fires and closed windows what the Glasgow bobby didn't manage with his cudgel. Sick people need fresh air as much as you do but you can get it outside and she can't.' And with that he turned Ian and Effie out like the rest.

The women stayed in a little cluster, their heads close and their tongues wagging. Fresh air! That would be mother's death! and they started recollecting all the people who had died from too much fresh air. But I was prepared to believe the wee doctor. If he ordered open windows then we must obey. Women! Weeping and wailing over the bed! That didn't do much good. They reminded me of a lot of hens disturbed by a hawk, all flustered and clucking.

Ian came over to me. 'How did you get hold of him, Sam? And how are we to pay him?'

I told him what had happened. 'The others can't pay either.'

Ian thought grandfather had a little money laid by but he didn't think the rest could pay.

'Didn't we ever have the doctor?' I asked, 'not even when

the little girls—' No, Ian told me, nearly everyone was sick then but no one had a doctor.

After that we waited and waited.

'He's been in a long time,' I said at last but just then he came out.

'Which of you is looking after the patient?' he asked and Effie hobbled forward so then he gave her instructions.

'Mind now! Plenty of fresh air and less of that fire!' were his final words to her. Then he came over to us.

'You've no sister? Pity now. Show me the way down and I'll tell you what I think.'

Once through the dyke he told us that Mother's heart was strong and her pulse steady. The blow had caused pressure on the brain. He could not be sure but he considered there was a fair chance that once the pressure eased she would regain consciousness.

'Now!' he said stopping to speak more clearly, 'if this happens you may find that her recollection is not perfect at first. She may live in past times but be unaware of what has happened recently. Now, if this is so—and I say "if" advisedly for I cannot foresee what will happen—but if this is so you must on no account worry her or try to make her remember. You will do her harm if you try but instead seize the chance to give her nourishing food, not tea and slops, but eggs and milk. Milk pudding too if you like but eggs especially. Don't sell them. Give them to your mother.'

Ian promised we would do exactly what he told us so then we walked on till we were above the Cuing and the doctor went to the edge and looked down.

'Was it here you had your wee fight? A good place, a good place. I'd have liked fine to see so many great gentlemen at a stand provided of course I was well clear of the stones myself!'

We hardly knew what to say and thought it safer to stay quiet. The question of a fee was weighing heavily on Ian and at last he brought the matter up. Would the doctor be so good as to give him time to pay? He'd go to the fishing and—but the doctor broke in.

'Time to pay? No, indeed, no such thing!' Then he saw our long faces and laughed.

'It's all right! It's all right. Philanthropists in Glasgow are paying my fees. They sent me a telegram begging me to visit all the wounded warriors in Braes. You're getting to be famous! And I dare say they might spend their money on many a worse cause! Provided those ruffians haven't fed my pony green grass!'

He seemed to have that pony of his very much on his mind for he cross-examined the boys on their behaviour threatening them with all kinds of awful punishments if Ginger foundered.

Then with a change of tone he said to us 'Keep a good heart! I've known cases of this kind make good recoveries and your mother is strong and healthy.'

With a friendly wave and a touch of the whip on Ginger's broad back he set off and seeing its head was towards its stable the pony trotted briskly.

12 *Prisoners' Return*

The news flashed round the townships—the prisoners were home! You may be sure I set off at a run but as I had the farthest to go I did not catch up with the crowd till they had reached grandfather's.

They made way for me to get through.

'Grandfather!' I cried.

'Is it yourself, Sam!' Why he wasn't looking any different just as if he'd newly come up from the beach after a spell out fishing!

'Oh! I'm glad you're back! Were they bad to you? Did they give you enough to eat? What did they make you do? Were you locked all the time in a wee cell?'

Grandfather's lean face crinkled into a smile. 'Talk of questions! but wait you, Sam, till we get inside—here's Peter's wife and his mother and—'

They came running to greet their men, laughing and crying with joy and I knew how they felt for I almost felt like crying myself I was so happy. Everyone was talking at once and no one was listening and then Peter and Seumas and Donald gave grandfather and Calum a kind of farewell salute and were carried along to their own homes and the noise died away.

Grandfather just stood there looking all round, at the croft and the sea and the sky. I didn't see that he need pay it so much attention. It was just the same as usual. I wanted him to hurry and answer all my questions. But he could not do that till grandmother calmed down. She was so pleased to see him she nearly ate him and only grew calm when grandfather said he was hungry and were the hens laying eggs?

'And what am I thinking of?' she exclaimed reproaching herself. 'Starving you must be and Calum the same way.' She examined Calum. 'You're thin! They didn't feed you well at all!'

This gave me a chance to get back to my question. 'What did they give you to eat?'

Grandfather's considered the question gravely. He was never one to give a hasty answer.

'Well, Sam, I've eaten worse at sea. They'd give us meat in the middle of the day, stew of some sort but I'll tell you one thing, Sam, they didn't dry the potatoes properly! You've seen your mother give the pot a shake over the fire after she's poured off the water? Well! I'm thinking they forgot that part in the prison. I thought of having a word with the cook.'

'And did you, grandfather?'

Everyone laughed and I realised grandfather was teasing but I was too happy to mind.

'But what made them let you go all of a sudden?' grandmother asked.

'I believe it was that telegram they sent from Peinchorran saying how behindhand the families here were with the spring work. When Mr Lucas read that—he was the governor and a very civil-spoken gentleman he was—he felt sorry for you all and the sheriff said we could get out on bail.'

I knew what bail was by this time so I asked how much they had to pay.

'Well! you'll hardly believe this, Sam, but they were wanting twenty-five pounds for every mother's son!'

That amazed us. Twenty-five pounds!

'When I heard that I said to myself you're finished, my lad. No one is going to pay twenty-five pounds for the likes of you, grey in the head and long in the tooth. Calum, there, or Seumas they might be worth the money—plenty of work in them yet but me!'

Everyone laughed except grandmother who said he was

worth every penny and more.

'But what did you do all the time?' I persisted longing to get a clear picture of this place prison.

'Well! I'll tell you, Sam, we did just what we do many a day at home.'

I didn't believe this. 'You're making fun of me.'

'Not me!' said grandfather. 'The five of us sat there mending nets and what with Calum on one side of me and Seumas on the other and a seagull up from the firth overhead I could believe myself here at home.'

'But the twenty-five pounds? Who paid that?'

'The good people of Inverness, the shopkeepers and Mr Mackenzie, Dean of Guild. They had it all collected by five o'clock yesterday evening and the warders hurried in to let us out. So there we were in the street in our working clothes, a tear in my trousers and Calum's elbow out through his jacket but we didn't let that worry us. Then Peter said "We've no money" and that was true. We hadn't a copper. Well, we stood there and we laughed. What did it matter? We were free.'

Calum took up the story. 'Father said "We'll walk! What's a hundred miles! We'll do it in three days." But Providence was still looking after us. These same friends who had gone bail for us came to take us to a hotel. Well, me with my jacket in tatters, I kept saying I was not fit to be seen inside a hotel but they said they would pay the bill and send along clothes more in keeping with a hotel than what we stood up in.'

'And so they did,' agreed grandfather, 'they treated us as if we'd been lairds and saw us off by the train this morning.'

'We had a right send off,' mused Calum, 'but it was nothing to what was waiting us in Portree and we had no expectations at all! Father was asking a sailor why there was such a crowd on the pier and was there some great man expected. Well! you could have knocked us down with a feather when he said it was us. I believe if we had been good at the swimming we'd have dived overboard and made for Peinfeilir. But we just had to stand there listening to the cheering. Then they got the gangway across and we held back thinking others should go first but no one would and the captain he came along and said to father, "Off you go, Alasdair, lead the way! Why be backward now?" '

'Aye, he's a grand man the captain. He would not carry the Glasgow—'

'Yes, yes, we heard but tell us what happened next?' I was helping grandmother with the meal seeing her arm was in a sling but I was listening to every word.

'Oh! nothing much. They lifted us up on their shoulders and carried us all the way from the boat to the Portree Hotel—'

'With a piper going ahead!' cried Calum slapping his knee with huge delight at the memory.

'Aye! but you tell me what he was playing!' chaffed Alasdair, 'no one could hear a note with the roaring of the crowd. He was wasting his breath, poor fellow!'

'Well it wasn't "Lochaber no more",' laughed Calum, 'that's certain and then when we reached the hotel and they let us down—and Peter and me we're no light weights!—we had to go in. We were as much prisoners as if we'd still been in the jail.'

'No one offers you a dram in jail,' reflected grandfather, 'and they gave us big drams and then they took to speech-making and they had a power of language but when it came to our turn we hadn't a word to say. "Thank you" was all we could manage between us! We were missing Neil! Now if he had been there he'd have given speech for speech but then it is a gift. But finally when they were all so busy miscalling Ivory and the landlords and had forgotten us we slipped away and it was great to have the road under our feet!'

'Yes,' agreed Calum, 'and smell the air. There is a sour smell in a jail which turned my stomach.'

By this time the meal was ready and we all ate and drank together and were happy. The house had filled up with neighbours anxious to hear the news and we had a great evening.

But it was different next day. I had hoped that Mother would know grandfather and that everything which had been awry since the day of the fight would be straightened out. But it was not to be. Mother paid no more attention to her father than to anyone else.

'If she won't eat she won't last long!' said Effie and that was just my own thought. I hated to look near the bed for it seemed to me that she grew smaller every day.

But two nights later when I was alone in the house (for Effie went home to her cats at night) Mother moved and muttered. At once I remembered the doctor's orders to give her food. Eggs, he had said, and milk. Milk was the quicker. I filled a mug but my hand shook so that some of the milk slopped over on the floor. I lifted Mother's head and said, 'Drink!' as loudly as I could. It was like a miracle when she drank a little.

I was so excited and pleased I determined to stay awake till Ian came but what with working all day I fell fast asleep on the hard bench.

When I opened my eyes it was to see Ian bending over the fire blowing it into life. I sat up.

'Ian!' I exclaimed.

'Aye! what is it, Sam? Why did you sleep on the bench?'

'I was waiting for you, I meant to stay awake to tell you—Mother! she drank some milk.'

'Drank some milk!' he repeated as if it was hard to believe. I told him exactly what had happened.

'Oh! that's good news, that's fine.' We looked at the bed.

The morning sun streaming in at the little window showed us Mother lying as still as ever.

'She did, Ian, she did drink.' I was afraid he did not believe me. 'There's the cup with the little she left in it!'

'Well, then, if she's come round once she'll come round again.' And he went back to making the breakfast but I stood staring down at Mother and noticed with a shock how white her hand had become. It lay outside the coverlet, no longer red and chapped. Her nails had grown smooth and long.

We were out all morning harrowing the ploughed land and all the time I was wondering when Mother would move again. I hurried home full of hope.

'Has she moved?' I asked the minute I was inside the door.

'Moved? No, indeed, and it's likely she'll not move any more in this world.'

'She did move! And she drank milk!'

'You're dreaming, boy! She has not stirred one inch since I came in.'

It was lucky that Ian came in at this moment, having stabled the pony or we would have been quarrelling.

'She came round for a wee while,' he told Effie, 'the doctor said it would take time. It's a beginning!'

'The doctor! The doctor!' grumbled Effie, 'he wants her to get her death of cold!'

Whenever she was alone she stuffed the broken window with rags. When we came in we took them out again.

Today, however, she let that be. She had other matters on her mind. When she had brewed a pot of tea she leaned over the table and said, 'When will you be coming to plough for me, Ian, a thasgaidh (which means treasure. Fancy being *her* treasure!) Now that Calum Alasdair is back you haven't their croft to do! You'll have time for poor Effie.'

I sat up fully expecting and looking forward to a row. Effie to ask us to plough for her when she had been meaning to pay the rent and do us down! Well, she had impudence, that one! Ian took his time answering while Effie sat stirring sugar round and round at the bottom of her mug.

'I'll plough for you when I can get Neil's pony along with

my own,' Ian said and I sat aghast.

'You're a good lad, Ian, a good lad to poor old Effie and it's your poor mother was good to her too!' and she lifted the corner of her apron to her eyes but I could have sworn they were as dry as my own.

'Why did you say that?' I asked angrily when Ian and I were outside standing close by the fallen rowan. The rowan was proof of Effie's treachery. It lay there and no one had even taken twigs off it for kindling.

'She's looking after Mother, Sam. What else could I say?' he asked reasonably but I could not be reasonable.

'She means us no good!'

'I'm not so sure,' he answered—he too was looking at the tree. 'Perhaps we acted a bit hasty that night!'

I stared at him in disbelief. How could he not *feel* that Effie wished us ill? He was big and strong and could do hundreds of things that I couldn't do but I knew in my bones that I was right about Effie and he was wrong. But he would not listen, not then nor later.

He was yoking the pony and only shook his head when I went on about it.

I was out with Archie one evening. He was making the round of his ewes. I had six lambs already and I was hoping he would not have more. He had six too but he said now that two of the ewes had still to lamb.

It cut me to the heart that Archie might beat me. Archie's sheep were grazing by the roadside. I took a good look at them and I couldn't see the ones he was talking about.

Archie moved slowly among them, his eye keen.

'That one, Sam!' and he pointed. Yes, all right, she did look like being in lamb but where was the other one? I couldn't see one. I shouldn't be so quick for two minutes after that Archie caught hold of another, turned her over on her back and sure enough there was milk in the udder. I wasn't a bit pleased and even less so when I saw grandfather on the road watching us.

'That's a nice ewe you've got there, Archie,' he said. Archie nodded. We stood looking at the sheep for a wee while and then grandfather turned and looked up at Ben Lee.

'The seventeen years will soon be passed,' he said musingly as he leaned on his stick.

'And what will we do, grandfather?' I asked eagerly.

He took his eyes away from the hill and smiled at me.

'We'll just put our sheep on,' he said and resumed his walk.

I set off after him. Archie and his sheep could look after themselves.

As we were nearing the schoolhouse the Master came out of the gate and waited for us. He and grandfather shook hands.

'I am glad to see you back, Alasdair,' said the Master in his formal way but he did not sound all that glad. He walked slowly up the road with us. He was stout and short of breath.

'It is a fine evening!' said grandfather and then we walked a while in silence.

But it was not like the Master to be silent for long. He coughed and cleared his throat and said, 'There is much news in the papers about us these days. We were better off when the newspaper did not concern itself with us!'

News of us? I ached to know what news but grandfather did not appear concerned. So eventually the Master had to tell him.

'The Member of Parliament for Argyll has asked the Prime Minister to set up a commission of inquiry into crofting to find out what substance there may be in those so-called grievances.'

A commission of inquiry. I had heard the words in the tailor's house. Now I longed for the Master to tell us more.

'That is news indeed!' said my grandfather, 'and what did Mr Gladstone reply?'

Whatever Mr Gladstone replied the Master took *his* time replying, partly because he needed his breath to walk up hill though it was not steep, and also because he was sorry things were going our way. He came to a stand among the birch trees and blew his nose. I longed to beg him to hurry up. At last he said that Mr Gladstone had not liked the question. There was already a motion on the order paper and the Government would do nothing till they had studied the matter.

This had me completely puzzled. What were order papers? Papers which gave orders? No, that couldn't be the answer.

Grandfather was not upset, however.

'I am sure the Government will do the best it can for us when it understands how we have been treated,' he said smiling at his old friend.

The Master made an indignant clucking noise.

'You should not let yourself be blown up with false hopes, Alasdair,' he said severely, taking a folded newspaper from his pocket. "It is not by violence and uproar and high-handedness that you will get justice." These are the words of a true Skyeman. Think it over, Alasdair. "It is not by violence and uproar and high-handedness that you will get justice!" These are wise words! And he says also "If you have any real cause of complaint there is no fear but you will get justice." '

Real cause of complaint! We had lost our hill. Was that not a real cause of complaint. I longed for grandfather to answer but he took his time.

'We have real cause of complaint, a Mhaighstir,' he said at last, 'and we did not act hastily. We petitioned the factor and when that failed we told him face to face we would not pay him the rent till he gave us back the hill. We used no violence till they tried to throw us out of our houses. We resisted eviction and then they brought a whole body of police to turn us out and we resisted these also. When we were peaceable we did not get justice.'

This was just what I wanted to hear and I could have shouted with joy but when I looked at the Master I could see he was struggling for words and that was not like him for he usually had long sentences rolling off his tongue.

'You—you are being led astray, Alasdair,' he groaned, 'and it grieves me, it grieves me, indeed it does. You, brought up in a Christian community should not follow the example of the Irish who cry "no rent" and lead campaigns of violence against their lawful superiors. If you do not take heed you will become as violent as the Fenians!'

Grandfather shook his head. The factor would get their rent as soon as they got the hill. Everyone had the rent ready.

The Master stopped. 'I have walked far enough. These spring winds are treacherous.' We waited expecting him to turn back but he made one more effort.

'You have been in prison already! Is prison not the one end to all your lawlessness? Are you so anxious to go back?'

Grandfather smilingly shook his head. 'No, no, I am not anxious to go back but I must serve whatever sentence they put upon me. But I am not ashamed! The Law has put good men in prison before now!'

'Alasdair! Alasdair! No man is good. We are all miserable sinners.'

'You are speaking the truth there, Master,' agreed grandfather politely, 'but we have a right to the hill.'

The Master's face went purple and all his chins wobbled.

'I have come too far,' he said and started back muttering, 'obstinate as an old mule.'

We walked on in silence. I was jubilant. I felt grandfather had had the best of that argument.

'Is a commission a good thing?' I asked him.

He considered this. 'I believe it is, Sam, for they will ask questions in public and then things which were done in secret will come into the light of day and the people who did these things will be sorry and ashamed. I believe a commission will give us justice.'

Would Angus Martin be ashamed? Or Norman Beaton who

had twisted my arm? It was hard to believe.

We had reached Lower Ollach and grandfather paused to stare over the crofts. I could not see that there was anything much to see, only men working, some harrowing, some sowing seed. Blue smoke was going up from all the fires for the women had gone home to make the evening meal. The cows were standing chewing the cud by the dyke waiting to be let in.

'But it was not justice I came out to get today but tobacco, Sam, for I haven't a pipeful left!'

We went through the gap in the dyke and crossed over to the little shop which sold tobacco, tea and sugar.

13 *I Am Deserted*

Ian made a fine row about the hens. He had told me to mend the bothy on the moor and take them there out of the corn seed and I had meant to do so but, good life, I was hard at it every hour of the day and small wonder I forgot.

'Send that dog of yours after them!' he growled so I sent Bess (I had called her Bess) and she soon chased them back where they belonged, but of course they'd come back as soon as she was out of sight. Ian told me I was no good, that I couldn't be trusted to do the least thing.

The upshot was that we collected the hens there and then and carried them over to the bothy in creels with sacks over the top.

When Ian saw the state the bothy was in with the branches sticking out through the turf he gave me the rough side of his tongue.

Then he got going with the spade and cut turfs. I carried them over and placed them on the framework of branches. Ian worked at such a pace the sweat ran off him and off me too but very soon we had filled up all the holes and the hut was as neat and tight as a bee's nest.

'There!' exclaimed Ian, wiping his forehead, 'they'll be snug enough now. The perches are all right and the creels for them to lay in. You'll have to come over twice a day to feed them. Promise me that, Sam. Mother needs the eggs.'

Yes, it was true, she was eating now but still she knew no one.

I had been gazing up at Ben Lee watching the cloud shadows crossing its green shoulder and I'd been seeing myself up there, my own sheep ahead of me, Bess at my heel.

My mind came back with a jerk to what Ian was saying. Promise? Why promise? But he was still talking.

'See and don't sell any of the eggs. Keep them for Mother. Tell Angus, the Shop, I'll pay the tea and sugar when I get home from the fishing.'

'Fishing!' I burst out. 'Oh! Ian you can't go, you can't. Mother's ill—there's no one—'

'I'll have to, Sam, I must earn money or how can we buy meal?'

I would not listen. 'Mother will die! That's what will happen. She's not right, she's not, she's not!'

Ian leaned on his spade and looked at me in astonishment.

'Good life! Sam, what's got into you? She's eating, she's getting up. It's only a matter of time, the doctor says.'

I did not believe him. The woman who ate and walked and sat on a chair was not my mother. But I could not say so.

'Black Murdo will come when you're away! He will! He will! He's after Maggie and he'll get the croft. They'll put us out and there'll be nobody here when you get home!'

'Aw! have sense, Sam. What is grandfather going to be doing when Black Murdo is turning you out? And Neil? Will they just stand by and watch?' and he laughed as if wanting me to laugh with him but I could not. Then he grew angry.

'You're behaving like a baby! Do you want me to sit at home holding your hand!'

That cut my pride. 'Baby!' I shouted. 'Who was the baby when you all turned tail at Penfeilir? Who went on to Portree to try to get grandfather out of jail?'

I was fair dancing with rage. As I grew angrier Ian grew calmer.

'All right! All right! I know you're not a baby. Well, act the man now, boy, and look after Mother when I'm away.' How did he not understand? That stranger was not Mother so why would I look after her? She had taken Mother's place and while she was there Mother could not come back!

I tried once more to explain but I felt the tears choking me and rushed away paying no heed to Ian's shouts.

Ian turfed the peat bogs before he left, taking two whole days at the job. It was hard work, the worst part of peat cutting and he was not willing to leave it to Donald.

On that last evening he told him that the bog was ready for cutting and that I would throw out for him. Oh! fine, a woman's job for me while he went sailing!

'Calum is off to the fishing already,' Donald remarked.

'I'm sailing with Angus of Cat's Cave. We'll be off with first light tomorrow.' My heart sank like a stone. I had hoped all the time that he would change his mind and stay at home this summer. Now I was sore against him and I went out so as not to have to speak to him.

The grass was wet with dew and glimmering in the summer dusk when I went home. I lit the lamp and saw Ian lying on the settle, fast asleep, his head on his arm and his boots still on his feet. I poured myself a mug of milk and he stirred, lay a moment staring at me and then sat up abruptly.

'Is it morning already?'

'No, I'm just going to bed.'

He stretched and yawned. 'Good life, I thought I'd slept all night and made Angus miss the tide.' He showed me an address he had written to which I could send if Mother got worse.

'Can you read it?' I nodded. For the life of me I could not talk naturally to him. I had sulked for so long. Much good knowing where he was would do me if Black Murdo came suddenly and Ian at the far side of the Irish sea! So I hugged my ill humour to me and went off to bed. When Ian came after me I had my back turned and let on I was asleep. I did drift off into a troubled slumber full of dreams. I was running hard to escape but I did not know who was after me. Then all at once I was in the crowded room in the

tailor's house and I was so glad to see Charles Ramsay. But
he had changed. He mocked me. 'You'll never get your
hill! You'll never have sheep! They'll shoot your dog!'
Such a heaviness came over me that I wept. If Charles
Ramsay deserted me who was left?

The slight noise Ian made getting out of bed woke me but
the black mood had me in its grip. I lay still, my head half
covered with the blanket but my ears told me what he was
covered with the blanket but my ears told me what he was
putting on his boots. He'd be wearing his blue fisherman's
jersey and navy blue jacket. I'd always thought him a picture
going off to the fishing and I remembered how Mother had
washed and cleaned for him days beforehand. No one had
done anything for him this time.

'Beannachd leat, a ghille' I heard him say which means 'a
blessing with you, boy!' and I heard the door shut. I sat
up, throwing off the blanket. I'd run after him, I'd tell him
I'd be all right, I'd look after everything when he was
away. I'd see him smile at me once more. I groped for my
trousers, pulled a jersey over my head and had my hand on
the latch when I stopped. Run after him? That was as much
as to say I'd been in the wrong and I hadn't. Mother was
just as ill as ever, Effie was not to be trusted. I could feel
blackness ahead but he only called me a baby! It was plain
I could not go. I sat down on the bed and presently wrapped
myself in the blanket and slept once more.

14 *Peat Cutting*

When Effie had milked the two cows we drove them ahead of us to the moor. The wind had gone to the north; sea and sky were blue and the sunshine dazzled the eye.

Most of the neighbours were already out. Uncle Donald used a peat iron to cut each peat out of the smooth side of the bog. I stood below and caught each one as it came loose and flung it out behind me. I'd often watched Mother doing this and saw her make a line as straight as if it had been ruled and I was sure I could do it equally well but to my disgust I threw some too far and others not far enough and some out of line altogether. And the weight of them! Well, they were light enough to begin with but they weighed with stooping and my arms with throwing out. The sweat ran down my forehead and made my skin smart and the back of my neck felt as if it were on fire. When I could bear it no longer I begged Uncle Donald for a rest. He stopped and stood there looking away at some distant hill while I longed for a word of encouragement and had to do without.

I could hear laughter coming from neighbouring banks, the deep voices of the men and the shrill voices of the women answering their banter and I marvelled how they had the breath for it. Not far off Chrissie, Archie's sister, was throwing out like an old hand but then she was two years older than me and besides it was women's work.

I took as many rests as I could till Uncle Donald got impatient. I longed for the midday break and when I saw the girls making a stone fireplace on the stance of an old peat stack I began to have hope. Soon they had made a good fire from old grass, twigs of dead heather and little bits of peat. The smell alone made me feel better. But if ever there was a slow kettle it was that one. It was huge and the fire burnt down and had to be renewed several times before it even began to sing. I could hear small children running around lightheartedly, chasing each other round old stacks and jumping the ditches. I remembered all the summers when I'd been doing that myself. I could run the fastest and jump the farthest of any of them.

At last they called us over. We made an effort to get the worst of the dirt off our hands by washing them in bog water but I didn't waste too much time over that and got myself a seat near the kettle. The tea when I got it although tasting of peat smoke was the best ever I had. It was a pleasure just to sit, my back to the wind and my face to the sun and the food itself, though Effie was no baker, tasted twice as good outside.

Neil was sitting near me and when he'd swallowed one cup of tea and stretched out for a second he took a look round and said, 'I've been hearing that Angus Martin, that fine fellow, has been getting threatening letters. Which of you has been worrying the worthy man?'

Ewen Nicolson of the croft below Neil's laughed so much that he choked over his piece.

'We are not so fond of letter writing! If we have a letter to write we go to the Master. I'm thinking he'd not be pleased if we wanted to threaten Angus!'

We all laughed heartily and then Neil went on 'I'm hearing the Portree people are afraid to sleep in their beds at night for fear the Braes men burn the roofs over their heads!'

'Well, did you ever,' exclaimed his wife, 'and us cutting peats. What time would we have for such foolishness?'

'Who can be putting such lies on us?' asked another.

To my dismay I heard my uncle's high-pitched voice break in.

'Perhaps they have good reason to fear violence. The

Braes people used it already against the person of the sheriff
officer when he was carrying out his lawful duty and not
content with breaking the law once they broke it a second
time assaulting the sheriff-principal himself.'

A growl came from the men and the women cried,
'Shame! Are you blaming your own father?'

Donald was sitting a little apart, his lank hair hanging
over his brow. He looked round the circle of angry faces.

'We are all sinful creatures!' he said steadily, 'fallen from
grace through the sin of our first father. We are led astray,
pushed by a puff of wind from the path of righteousness. My
sister pays the price of disobedience to God's will! Yes and
if we do not repent, punishment will fall on us also as it
has fallen on her!'

Ignoring their angry protests he got to his feet, removed
his cap and asked a blessing on the food they had eaten.
Then he walked slowly to the peat bank.

I was crimson to the ears. How could my uncle talk like
that? Why had he always to be different? Scraps of angry
talk reached me. 'Wants us put out of our houses!—Let
his own father go to prison without lifting a hand—blames
us and not *them*—Mhairi Alasdair hurt no one—'

I couldn't lift my head to look at them. In a little while
they all went back to work but I sat on. I would not, no, I
would not work with *him*! He had shamed me in front of
the neighbours. But presently I became aware that Neil was
still there.

'Grand weather for drying the peat!' he remarked. 'If
this north wind lasts we can have it all stacked inside
three weeks.' He knocked the dottle out of his pipe and
added in an offhand way, 'You're not working for *him*, lad,
but for your mother. She'll need fires to keep her warm in the
winter.'

I knew Neil had the truth of it but still I muttered, 'I can't
work with him! I won't go near him.'

Neil shook his great head. 'Ah! well, there's worse than

Donald, the kind that speak you soft to your face and miscall you to your back! Your uncle doesn't do that and give him his due, it takes courage to speak out against the rest.'

I couldn't see that at the time but his first argument made its way with me. I got reluctantly to my feet sure that everyone was either condemning or pitying me—and I didn't know which was worse—and slouched back to my place in the bog to throw out peats the whole of that day.

15 *Jean Has Her Say*

Donald had one last go at me to bring me over to his way of thinking.

It was his last evening at home. He was going the next day to be a catechist in Rona. We were both tired after a hard spell in the peats. When we had finished supper he said, 'I am leaving home now and you will be in charge—'

'Effie's in charge!' I interrupted crossly. 'She's in charge. You'd think it was *her* house!'

We were always having rows about the bitch. She didn't want Bess inside the house and I wasn't going to leave her out.

'She can't even cook!'

A kind of wintry smile crossed his face. 'We should not concern ourselves with the inner man, Sam!'

But why not? It was as easy to cook well as to cook badly, wasn't it? But I didn't bother to say so and he went on, 'I want you to stay close to the house! We do not know when your mother may come to her senses and there should be someone of her own near her on that day!'

Well! if he thought so why did he not stay himself? Why should it always be me?

'You have been much abroad lately—'

But this was too much. 'I've been working in the peats!'

'But before that you were hardly ever indoors! We hardly saw you from morn to night!' He said this in a patient, long-suffering kind of voice which did nothing to sweeten it to me.

'Samuel! I am leaving home but your salvation is near to my heart. I beg you to turn away from worldly things and

worldly strife. These things have no lasting value! Set your
heart on the one thing that matters—your road to Heaven! If
you will only do that, Sam, you will find such happiness
that all earthly pleasure will fade into insignificance—'

What earthly pleasures did he think I had? Effie's sodden
potatoes, sour oatcake, clacking tongue! I had had pleasures
when Mother was—was—alive and we had laughed and
joked together and she could make a fried herring into a
feast but that had all gone.

'I've got to go and have a last look at the sheep,' I
mumbled, 'and give Bess a run. She's been tied up all day.'

The eager look went out of his face but he stepped out of
my way and I escaped outside. He had gone by the time I got
up in the morning.

So that left me and Effie.

'Two cuddies! Is that all you could catch. You're a poor
fisherman.'

'It's the north wind! You don't get good fishing with a
north wind.'

She took one of them herself and fried the other for
Mother. All I had was potatoes.

She began about them. 'You'll need to stay at home and
take the sprouts off them or they'll go soft.'

That was one thing I would not do! The way she cooked
them it was all one, were they hard or soft to start with.

She was good at scolding. But there were other times
when she would tell me the inside stories of families in
Braes. She had something bad to say about nearly everyone. She had not done this when Uncle Donald was at
home. She was just that little bit in awe of him but now she
came out with old quarrels over stealing peats or taking oars
out of a boat or stealing hens.

There's no point in denying that I liked listening and yet
afterwards I would have a sour taste in my mouth.

Things went on in this way for a while. Then one day I
remember I was waiting for Mother to finish her food for

I wanted the scraps to give to Bess. For this reason I was watching her and I noticed how much stronger she was but I kept catching an odd look on her face. I sat puzzling myself where I had seen such a look before and all of a sudden it hit me. She was just like a small child, not sure whether to expect a kind word or a scolding. It was Effie she looked to. When Effie said, 'Get up!' she got up and when Effie said, 'Go to bed!' she went.

But why? Why did she have to go in fear of Effie? There was no understanding it. I sat fondling Bess's ears and wishing Mother would hurry up. The minute she stopped eating I had the plate on the floor. Effie gave a screech.

'Give me that for Tomas! He's half starved, the poor beast!'

The more starved Tomas was the better I'd be pleased but indeed he caught so many mice he was as sleek as a seal. I stood over Bess who was a very finicky eater so that Effie couldn't snatch the plate. She made a pot of tea grumbling the while.

When it had drawn she poured out a cup, put her hand over it and said, 'Ask me for it, a Mhairi, and you'll get it.'

Mother put out her hand smiling uncertainly. She liked her cup of tea but Effie shook her head.

'Say "Effie, I want my tea." Say it, now!'

It was plain she could not. She drew back her hand and her lip trembled putting me in mind of a disappointed child.

I sprang up, snatched the tea pot and poured her out a cup. 'There! There's your tea.'

'You mind what you're doing!' stormed Effie. 'Who's looking after her I'd like to know? What do you ever do for her, out stravaiging morn and noon and night! A fine time she'd have with you!'

I flushed and stammered. 'I'd look after her all right if you—if you—'

Effie gave her cackle of a laugh. 'Oh! to be sure, you'd be real good to her if I wasn't here! Well! I'll away home to my cats, they're missing me bad and Tomas himself doesn't like this house.'

'You know fine I can't stay in all day! There's the sheep—'

'You'll be tired out looking after them, all ten!' says she very sarcastic.

'And I'll be lifting the peats soon, they're drying grand—' I hurried on aghast at the thought of being left.

'I'm needing peats this minute,' she said in a different tone, 'but don't come home with a puckle at the bottom of the creel! Put a top on the creel like your mother did. What's the matter with you? You've no more strength than a girl!' She dipped her oatcake in the tea till it was soggy and then chewed it with her gums. 'If the little girls had lived they'd have been good to their mother! But what's the use of a boy?'

It wasn't a question and I did not answer. I wouldn't let her see I minded.

'Get your mother some carrageen, Sam. Take her cup and I'll fill it again.'

I took Mother's cup and as I did so I realised what it was in Effie's way of talking that I did not like. She behaved as if Mother was not there or was an imbecile like Donald Ban in Balmeanach. I told Mother I'd get her carrageen. She'd like that, wouldn't she?

'I'll make her a pudding of it,' said Effie, 'she was always fond of that. I wonder how the fishing is doing. It's strange there's no word coming from Ian.'

'He never does write.'

'Maybe he didn't when your mother was well but when she's so poorly it's very strange him not writing.'

She was squinting up at me and I wondered uneasily what she was hinting at. Ian hated pen work just as much as I did. She stirred her second cup of tea. 'He'll be writing someone else! That'll be the way of it!'

'Write someone else? Who?'

She had a laugh like the grating of an unoiled hinge.

'That's the way of it, Sam! We bring them into this world in sorrow and pain and work our fingers to the bone to bring them up and then when they're big and strong and could be a help—' she stopped short and took to stroking Tomas's broad back.

What made her stop there? Who was she talking about? I asked, annoyed by this round and round business.

'You just ask yourself, Sam, who is he making the money for?'

'Ask myself that! I don't need to!'

'Och! Tomas, is he not far back? Hasn't his brother been courting Angus of Cat's Cave's daughter this year and more on the quiet, meeting her in the bay in the early morning and him back from the fishing!'

And suddenly I saw it all. Jean! Jean smiling at me, Jean blushing over the little wooden dolls and running away. What a fool I'd been not to guess! Ian would come home with a pocket full of golden sovereigns—all for Jean! My mother and I must do without.

I looked at Mother to find that she was rocking herself backwards and forwards. It was almost as if she understood her loss.

'Now see what you've done!' cried Effie quick to put the blame on me. 'Off you go and get those peats. She's better alone with me. You just upset her!'

I knew very well I hadn't upset her but I didn't stay to argue. All I wanted was to get outside and away from Effie. If I could have done without food I'd never have gone home.

I picked up the creel and with it slung over my shoulder and Bess at my heel I made for the hill. The wind had left the north at last. The air was mild and soft, full of the scent of bog myrtle. Tormentil starred the grass with its tiny yellow flowers, bog cotton waved its silken tassel in the breeze and the wheatears, summer visitors to us, flitted ahead of me giving out their chack! chack! cry. I saw and heard all this but none of it could move the load of misery I carried worse by far than any load of peat. I filled the creel full putting the top layer standing upright, half their length above the top. I had trouble rising with this load on my back and was half dead with the weight of it before I reached home but Effie's jibes kept me to it. At the side of the house I let the load down and slid my head out of the rope. I was dizzy with the effort, sweating and trembling and my arms sore from the chafing of the rope. When I had got my breath back I made down for the shore. The tide was out and I soon had a full bucket of carrageen and climbed up the bank with it meaning to go straight home but the very thought brought a darkness down on my mind. I lay face down on the grass pressing my face into it wishing I could stop thinking and feeling. I could hear the herring gulls overhead and the plaintive cry of the sandpipers down on the wet sand. I remembered Jean telling me how much she loved them.

'Sam!' It was as if thinking of her had made her come. I jumped to my feet. 'Well, aren't you the big stranger,' she said as she had said that day so long ago, 'where have you been all this time?'

She knew well enough I was just at home. Where else would I be?

'Don't go away! Isn't it lovely here? I thought you were asleep when I saw you first. What have you got there? Oh! carrageen, do you like it?'

'It's for Mother.'

'Oh! yes, of course. We're so glad she's better. What a blessing she can eat now, Sam!'

All the old women who came to the house said the same thing! Wasn't it wonderful to see her so well! and her cheeks so red! When I saw them coming now I ran the other way. I'd had my fill of people saying she was coming on wonderfully when she was no more than a stranger.

'She's—she's—not herself!' I muttered staring at the ground.

'Oh! I know, Sam,' she murmured in her soft voice, like

I

music in my ears, 'I know what you must be feeling but I'm sure she'll—she'll come back.'

She was the only person who seemed to understand but I did not want her sympathy. I could only stand awkwardly there as if bereft of the power to walk away.

She had sat down and was picking daisies, stripping them of their petals. We were both silent till Jean pointed out to sea saying, 'Oh! look, the *Glencoe*. She's early to-night. We had a letter from father yesterday and he says the fishing is good this year.'

I looked at the long prow of the *Glencoe* appearing from behind Aird. Then I looked down at her.

'Your father can't write!' and felt anger burn in me like a dull fire.

'No, but someone wrote it for him,' she replied and blushed, 'that's the way he always does.'

I had a tight feeling in my throat.

'It was Ian who wrote *you* and he did not write us.' There! I'd got it out. Now it was up to her but all she said was 'Well! he's not very good with a pen, no, no, I mean he doesn't like writing but he can write a good hand when he starts!' and she smiled up at me as if asking me to agree.

'He wrote you but he did not write us!' I repeated dourly. She jumped to her feet.

'Oh! Sam, what's the matter with you? Your brother's away working hard for you and your mother and all you can do is keep up some petty grievance against him! You wouldn't even—you didn't say goodbye but let him go without one kind word!'

So she knew that too! So she knew everything! Ian didn't care what bad things he told her about his own brother! All right then!

'He's not working for us!' I shouted red with anger. 'He's working for you!'

I was not ready for what happened next. She came at

me, her eyes flashing and I ducked thinking she was going to box my ears.

'Do you know what you are, Sam Nicolson,' she stormed and her voice went low with anger, 'a nasty spoilt boy thinking of no one but himself. That's what you are, just that!'

I stood gaping so startled I hadn't a word to say but even if I had she wouldn't have listened. 'How dare you say such things about your brother? He's worked since he was a wee lad to help his mother. He's taken more and more on his own shoulders. And as for *you*—you wouldn't even do your share. Many a time Ian's gone home to find you haven't gone for the cows and you've left your mother to carry all the water. She spoilt you, of course. Maybe it wasn't altogether your fault. She'd lost the little girls so she made too much of you. But I'm telling you it's time you grew up and stopped acting like a ten year old. And now you take offence because Ian wants to marry me? Is that it? Is that the big crime? Well! I'll tell you straight we do want to marry, but that doesn't mean he'll desert his mother. It means just the opposite. It means I'll look after her if—if she needs me and if not—well! I hope she won't take against me—' her voice broke and she ran away leaving me there, my head in a whirl.

16 *The Ponies*

The ponies, mine and Archie's, were standing by the gate in the dyke.

'They're not looking great!' Archie remarked. That was true enough. They were in poor shape, their ribs showing, their coats matted and rough. Now that the work was over they needed good grazing and my eyes went to the hill.

'Come on! Let's put them out!'

'Right! There's nothing for them inside the dyke.' Archie opened the gate and we clambered up, he on Tommy and me on Sally and away we went. For all they were looking so poorly they moved at a fair pace climbing the hill till we were looking over moorland and on to distant hills and sea and felt ourselves the lords of creation. An eagle hovered over us and then made off with slow, heavy wing beats, up, up to the high hill.

'Bad for the lambs!' said Archie.

'Good hunting to it! They're Black Murdo's lambs!'

When we had gone a good way we jumped down and left the ponies in a green hollow. The last we saw of them they had their heads down as if time was short. I challenged Archie to a race and had all I could do to keep up with him—well, his legs were longer than mine. We lay panting in the heather and the two dogs lay a little way off watching us.

'She's getting good, Archie! I drive the sheep up the hill every morning. You should just see them make off the moment they hear me whistle. They don't wait to see her!'

'It's not good for a young dog to learn driving away first,' said Archie, his long face thoughtful, 'you should be teaching her to bring them in to you.'

'I know that as well as you! But what can I do? She's the

only dog I've got. When we have our own sheep I'll teach her right.'

'She'll have got into bad habits by then.'

Archie had a way of coming out with things I didn't want to hear. I was fair annoyed. Bad habits or not I'd go on driving Black Murdo's sheep away. Murdo had killed Ben and I hadn't forgotten. Archie's voice cut in on my thoughts.

'They're just falling down on the other townships, the boys were telling me. Get them to chase the sheep away as well!'

'You're right, Archie! I'll do just that.' And I did. It was just what I needed, some ploy to take me out of myself. The boys were as keen as mustard so every morning at first light and long before the sun had shown himself over Raasay I would drive the flock fast and far right up the steep flank of Ben Lee. Bess became good at routing out every stray and straggler from behind knolls and out of hollows while far off on my left I could see other flocks moving upwards.

'It's queer, isn't it, Archie, here I am chasing the sheep every day and no one says a word to me and yet when I only put Ben round them that day what a row there was! How do you explain that?' Archie took his time over that one.

'Maybe it was the fight and the men being put in jail and then all the talk.'

That was a whole lot of reasons! Not that I minded what caused the change so long as I had my own way.

I wasn't thinking only of sheep you may be sure. There was one bit of my mind that went over and over what Jean had said to me—over and over—and I could see her and hear her voice and I wished I could do neither. It used to hit me at night when I was falling asleep. I was angry with her at first. What business had she to say I was spoilt and selfish? Me! and all the work I did! Besides she'd got hold of the wrong end of the stick entirely. *I* wasn't spoilt, I was only a second best, a stop gap for Mother when she lost the little girls.

And yet, and yet, as time passed small things popped up into my memory. Oh! trifles, just, the time when I'd gone off fishing and left my work to Ian, the time I'd refused to lift potatoes for Mother when I wanted to play with the boys.

It was fair torment lying in the dark remembering and then that last night—I hadn't even said a kind word nor wished him God speed and because of that he might never come back. The sea would have him too as it had had my father. I'm telling you I was unhappy and worst of all why had I let Effie poison me against Ian and Jean? It wasn't as if I didn't know Effie's way of running everyone down. Why in the world had I not taken time to think before blurting out that rubbish? Sometimes at night I pictured myself seeking Jean out and asking her to forgive me but in daylight I lacked the courage. So I worked off my unhappiness on the sheep.

Then Neil heard that we had let the ponies out.

'What were you meaning?' he roared at us, 'we'll be lucky if we see them alive!'

But I didn't mind Neil shouting at me the way I used to.

'We're going to put the sheep out soon so why not the ponies?'

'Because they wander! Sheep stick to their own ground. Any fool knows that!'

He filled his pipe and took a pull at it. It must have soothed him for presently he shrugged and chuckled, 'Have it your own way. That's how it used to be, all the horses roaming the hill all summer. It was a job finding them sometimes.'

But it was a different story two days later. I went all unsuspecting to find Neil in a fury with a letter from John Mackay, the butcher. He'd pounded the ponies and demanded a pound for each before he'd let them go.

'A pound! A pound!' Neil bellowed, glaring at me, 'see what you've done now. A pound! You just tell me how I'm to pay a pound, eh? Eh? Eh?' and with each repetition he pushed his angry face closer to mine.

This was terrible news. I had no pound nor yet the half of one. We weren't even paying the sugar and tea we were getting. Neil's rage went blasting over my head like a south-west gale coming off Glamaig. Archie was sitting dumb.

When Neil ran out of breath I asked where the ponies were. That set him off again (as I knew it would) but I had to know. What good would it do if he told me—I was too fond of my own way!—I'd live to be hanged and so on but at last he came out with it—the ponies were in Glenvarri-gill, Lachlan Ross's farm. Lachlan Ross! I remembered him all right! He was the one who had brought out the Volun-teers and spoilt our plans.

'Will they be in the fank?'

But this was one question too many. Neil's temper boiled over. How did he know where they'd be. Wherever they were—supposing it was the Royal Hotel they were in!—he couldn't get his without paying a sovereign. That's what I'd let him in for! He got up and stalked off into the house and all the children who had been cowering behind bushes during the storm, came out gazing at me in awe.

'You didn't say a word!' I told Archie, 'and this time you were just as keen to let them out as me but you let your father put all the blame on me!'

'I did not! I told him just what happened but he wouldn't listen. It's a calamity! I'll never hear the end of this—'

'It wasn't you he was on to!'

'Oh! he'll be on to me next and I'm here all the time. What on earth can we do, Sam?'

I took a look round at the ring of goggling children.

'Come on! We'll have a talk somewhere a bit private!'

When we were well away I said, 'We'll fetch them back ourselves!'

'Och! Sam, how can we? They'll be watched!'

'Not all night! Of course they won't. Who's going to stay

awake just for that?'

But I had a job getting him to come. First he held out because the night was too bright. What we would need was a dark night. Then he couldn't be out all night without his mother taking alarm and sending the whole township out after him. I told him to make up a story that he was going poaching.

In the end he agreed but with so little liking that I was afraid he would cry off.

I waited on the hillside as nervous as a kitten for what seemed an age but at last just as I was thinking of setting off alone he came saying, of course, right off that it was far too bright a night for our purpose. I didn't argue the point. We'd see when we reached the fank what we could do and meantime there was no sense in worrying.

We kept to the road but slipped off into the heather when we heard someone coming, so no one saw us. When we had passed several townships we turned off the road and followed a track across the moor which brought us out at the bridge near Glenvarrigill farm house.

For some time I'd been watching a black cloud swelling up over the hill above the farm.

'See that? We're going to be lucky!' I whispered. We followed the bed of the river as it ran its last half-mile on its way to the sea in Portree Bay. Opposite the fank we halted. We could see lights in the farm house but luckily a good bit away from us.

By now the cloud loomed blue black and was spreading wider and wider. There would be a thunder plump soon. We came out of the shelter of the river bank and made a dash for the fank, doubled up. We crouched beside the rough stone wall, panting. So far so good and now for the ponies. We kept close to the wall till we reached a big wooden gate. I could hear munching and breathing and was sure we had found the ponies till I heard a bleat. Bother! it was sheep I'd heard. The fank was full of them.

We'd have to try further on. We hadn't gone ten paces when we heard a whinny and scrabbling noises and a fall of small stones.

They were right beside us but there was no gate. We climbed up easily as there were niches in the wall to put our toes in. From the top we looked into the catching fank and and there they were. Sally was up on her hind legs and first I thought she was trying to get out but then I saw she was trying to reach grass growing on top of the wall.

'They're starving!' I heard Archie whisper. It was on the tip of my tongue to say *you* didn't want to rescue them! when I smelt tobacco. I grabbed Archie and pulled him down into the deepest shadow. The ponies had made so much noise scrabbling with their hoofs that we hadn't heard the men. Lucky I have a good nose.

'A good gathering!' one said and I judged he must be at the gate.

'Good enough!' With a shiver I recognised Black Murdo's voice. My heart sounded loud as a ship's engine in my ears. They'd be bound to hear it!

'Aye! we'll have them sheared this time tomorrow if the weather holds.'

There was a silence. I imagine they were leaning on the gate smoking. Then the first man said he didn't like the look of the clouds. There was a change brewing.

'A shower maybe, no more.' Black Murdo said and again there was silence. It was worse than talk. Just suppose they took it into their heads to look at the ponies! I'd got an arm twisted under me and the longer I lay the more it ached but I did not dare move.

And then they began to talk and I became so interested listening I forgot my cramped, painful position.

'I am not understanding it one bit!' Black Murdo said suddenly. 'No! it was never like this before. My sheep getting no rest and yet the factor won't do a thing! Did you ever hear the like in all your born days?'

'Perhaps he doesn't know about it—'

'With Mackay telling him every other day! Mackay is saying if this was a landlord's sheep the crofters were harrying he'd be down on them like a ton of bricks but seeing he's only a butcher it doesn't matter!'

'But there's a law in the land!' said the other. 'It's not right taking to do with another man's sheep!'

'Isn't that just what Mackay told him, face to face! and him sitting there behind his big desk and all he could say was, "Wait, Mackay, wait." But last time John told him he'd not renew the lease. Ben Lee wasn't keeping a coat to his back the way things were!'

'And what did Alasdair Ruadh say to that?'

'Oh! he just sighed sort of and said John had been a good tenant, always up to date with the rent and he'd be sorry to lose him. Mackay wanted him to say he'd deal with the crofters but no, he hadn't a word about them! So I'm to lose my job because he's gone soft! And I've been a good shepherd all my days and I've never broken the Law but it's me that will suffer.'

Sally whinnied. 'Time they came for these ponies! If they don't come soon they'd better bring spades!'

His crony laughed at this bit of wit and then the rain came down in a torrent.

'We'll have to run for it!' We stayed stock still till the last sound of their going had been swallowed up in the swish of the rain. Then we got to our feet brushing the dried horse dung from our jerseys.

'Did you hear that? Mackay going to give up the hill?'

'I heard him. Hie! catch Sally.' No time to talk just now. We bridled them and led them into the big fank, the sheep rising and scattering as we came through it. It was dark enough now. Archie gave me Tommy's rope to hold while he opened the gate. Then he jumped on his back and made off. I dragged the heavy gate with one hand holding Sally with the other. She was panting to follow Tommy and strained at the rope. I tried again and got the gate over a few feet. Why hadn't Archie waited? I thought resentfully and then I had an idea. I'd leave the gate open!

I jumped on to Sally's back and away she went to find Tommy. He had his head down and was busy eating and she followed his example. So there we were, two hundred yards from the farm house and sitting ducks for anyone looking out. No! the rain was as good as a curtain while it lasted.

Archie was struggling with Tommy, hitting him with his heels and tugging at his head but to no purpose. The beast was starving and was going to fill its stomach in spite of him. I could have wept. Everything had gone my way but now in sight of victory the stupid animals were going to let themselves be caught once more. As to what would happen to us well! it didn't bear thinking of.

We dragged them inch by inch down to the river. At once they put their heads down and drank in that slow way horses have as if sieving the water through their teeth. I kept looking at the sky and seeing it grow lighter every minute.

'Hold Tommy!' Archie went searching for a switch of willow, one for me and one for himself.

We mounted once more on the far bank of the river and then we slashed at them with the switches as hard as we could. To our joy they broke into a canter and we had no trouble getting them on to the track and following it in the half dark. At the crest of the moor I looked back. Not a light showed. I gazed hard at the fank. Was that something white coming out of the gate? I could not be certain and wished I'd taken the time to drive the sheep out but I'd been in too much of a panic, my one idea to get clear away.

I whipped up Sally alongside Archie. 'I left the gate open!' He stared at me, mouth open. 'You what?'

But he'd heard me all right. I just grinned.

'You're out of your mind, boy! They'll be after us with daylight.'

'They'll be after us anyway!' And I laughed. I'd worried

enough for one night. Now I didn't care. I'd got the ponies out from under Black Murdo's nose and I was on top of the world feeling wonderful riding home with the sweet smell of the earth after rain in my nostrils, feeling the mare's muscles bunch under me as she leaped a narrow stream. I was a king, afraid of nothing and no man and all at once Archie, solid and sedate as he was, started to laugh.

'Black Murdo! Wish we could see his face when he gets to the fank gate tomorrow!'

'Today!' The rain had stopped and we could make out from the height of the road the grey glimmer of the sea locked in by black hills. When we rode through the birch copse in Ollach a thrush fluted and fell silent.

'We'll take them to Aird,' said Archie. 'We can hobble them out of sight and Black Murdo will never think of looking there.'

The very place! So just as the sky grew light in the east we cantered out on the green banks above the bay and as we reached the far side colour flamed upwards from palest pink to deepest crimson.

Out of sight of any house we slid off the ponies' backs and made hobbles out of the rope reins and so we left them.

At grandfather's house Archie left me. The old dog growled hearing our footsteps but I spoke low to him when I went in so then he thumped his tail to the earthen floor. I stretched myself out beside the fire and fell asleep the next moment.

17 *Black Murdo Again*

I woke up and staring at the curtain of the box bed wondered where I was. Then I heard grandmother scolding Tweed for getting under her feet and I remembered my adventures. I came out to find grandmother testing the potatoes with a knitting needle to see were they cooked.

'And is that you awake at last! I thought you were one of the seven sleepers! What have you been up to, Sam?'

I was just going to tell her the whole story when grandfather came in rubbing his hands and chuckling.

'So you got them! Good for you, Sam! He's a chip off the old block!' he added addressing grandmother, 'Poor Angus! Many a ploy he was up to.'

'What are you talking about, Alasdair?' asked she quite cross at not being in the know.

'He got the ponies out of the fank. Mackay had pounded them. Two days with nothing to eat.'

'The rascals! You did very well, Sam, and they can whistle for their money.'

'But that's not all! Tell her the rest, Sam!'

I had been meaning to glide over that part of the night's work thinking grandfather would be annoyed but I could see he was not going to scold. But all I said was that I'd left the gate open.

'And what if you did! That was the best thing you could do for they'd think the beasts got out by themselves.'

'Aye! and the sheep too!' observed grandfather.

'Sheep!' her voice changed. 'Oh! Sam, what have you been up to?'

She was holding the potato pot and with the worry she

was in I was feared she'd scald herself letting the pot tip
to one side.

'He's done grand. But pour the water off those tatties and
give us our dinner. Sam and me had best go fishing.'

Grandmother went out hastily with the pot. Now she was
in a hurry to have us out of the house as quick as possible.

But I was hungry and you can't just belt fish or you'll
end up choking on the bones.

'It's all right, woman, it's all right!' Grandfather kept
saying. 'I've a sentry posted. So soon as Black Murdo shows
his face at Neil's we'll have word of it.'

'And what if he comes here first? What good will your
sentry be then?'

'Why would he come here? Maybe he'll go to Sam's house
but he'll not come here. You did the right thing, boy. Make
the tea, Sarah.'

Grandmother was like a hen on a hot girdle, going out and
coming in and telling us to hurry, hurry. It struck me she
must be remembering that April morning when the warning
was too late. I was trying to tell grandfather what I had
heard Black Murdo saying about the factor when she came
running saying Black Murdo had reached Neil's and we
must leave instantly.

'Time enough! Time enough! Neil is not the man to be
hurried—Aye! you were saying, Sam?'

But my grandmother's nervousness had infected me by this
time and I said I'd tell him all about it on our way to the
boat. And where was Archie? Did he know?

'He went off for a load of wood to Raasay. The proprietor
is very free with his wood—he's a real gentleman.'

We were out in the bay before we got back to what
Black Murdo had said. Grandfather was very pleased and
made me repeat it over and over.

We were on the fishing bank between Aird Point and the
Black Rock. We could see Neil's house and croft plainly but
my own house standing farther back on its ledge was not

in sight. We were too far off in any case to make out people moving.

I wasn't worrying. I felt I had done my share with Archie's help and I could leave the rest to the men. They'd know what to do. I was wonderfully contented sitting there baiting my hook with mussel and throwing out the line. The only drawback was that grandfather was a very impatient fisher- man. If he did not get a bite almost the moment a hook went overboard he'd be telling me to haul up the anchor and that anchor was no mean weight. I'd stand with one leg on the thwart and the other on the seat and pull and heave with the salt water spraying off the rope on to my legs. If I left it half-way up the boat was hard to row but if I took it right in then my back ached. Och! I didn't mind really only I believe with a wee bit more patience we'd have caught just as many fish on the one spot.

At last at slack water we gave up and rowed for the bay round the back of Aird. I saw the ponies grazing and a boy near them. Grandfather nodded. Yes he had posted one there as well. Boys helped us pull up the boat and we heard that Murdo had gone home. Seumas Mor had seen him striding off, his face as black as a thunder cloud and his two dogs sneaking along behind. Neil had been one too many for him.

But when I reached grandfather's I knew I must hurry home. I'd been away for too long. After all I was the man of the house.

Grandfather offered to come with me but I told him not to bother. Grandmother said Mother might be missing me. They gave me a string of fish and I set off. Missing me! Oh! no, she did not miss me. She did not even know me so how could she miss me? As I walked I felt the old load come down on my shoulders.

If it hadn't been for the dogs I'd have walked straight into trouble. Two black brutes came leaping at me. Now I'd heard that dogs won't attack a man lying down. I dropped in my tracks. I had not a minute to lose. With the din they were making Black Murdo (for these were his dogs—I knew them fine) Black Murdo would be on top of me. I took the one look round. There wasn't a hiding place of any sort. I was in the slight hollow at the edge of the corn field. The corn was a little over a foot high so what with the hollow and it waving beside me I was hid from anyone unless he came right close. But why would he not with the clamour the dogs were making? He'd come, nothing surer and lying there my heart failed me.

I could see nothing, my nose to the earth but I could hear. He had come out. He'd be on top of me in a moment. My fingers gripped a clod near me, not to let fly with it but just to have something to hold on to. And then behind me the corncrakes started up. They come and nest in our corn every summer and when it's cut we see where the nest has been. They make a great noise at night. I wondered was this the last time I'd hear it.

And then—I could hardly believe my ears—I heard Murdo call the dogs off.

'Are you barking at corncrakes now?' They slunk away, tails between their legs.

I was shivering like an aspen. That was a near thing! If it hadn't been for the corncrake he'd have come over to see what they had found. I'd never try and find a corncrake's nest again.

When I was over the worst of my terror I began to think. Should I go for Neil, send word from there to grandfather? That would have been the best plan and the safest. There was only one thing against it and that was the curiosity which was eating me up. I wanted to discover what Effie was plotting with the shepherd. I raised my head and saw a gleam of firelight coming from the tiny window in the thatch at the back of the house. If I could reach the window I could use my old tunnel in the thatch to hear what they were saying. I'd know then for sure whether Effie meant to try and put us out. I got cautiously to my knees and at once the bigger of the two black brutes was back, growling in his throat, the hair at the back of his neck rising. Much use me thinking of spying on Murdo or of getting help. I could do neither. I was a prisoner! It looked as if I'd have to lie on the bare ground all night and already I felt the chill of the falling dew. The fish gleamed in the dusk. Fish! Of course, I was a fool and no mistake. I got hold of the string and slipped the first fish off. Once more I got to my knees and once more the dog was on top of me. I threw him the fish as quick as I could and ran for the back of the house, loosening a second fish as I went. That one went to the second dog. Good life! His jaw closed on it. It would not last him a moment. I wished they'd choke themselves.

I was there! Now for the window. What if they suddenly noticed my head against the pale evening sky? I'd try the hole first. I put my ear to it and at once heard voices but could not make out what they were saying, partly because of my own heartbeats and partly I realised presently because Murdo's speech was slurred and indistinct. It had a very strange sound coming out from the dark.

Next I peered through the tiny window and when my eyes had become accustomed I could make out the thick figure of a man crouched over the fire. The flames lit up his craggy features, made his eyesockets into shadow-filled hollows, showed his beetling brows and the sweep of rough black hair. Effie I could not see but when I put my ear to the tunnel I heard her clearly.

'You see how it is, Murdo, a ghraidh,' she was crooning. 'It's the work of Providence. The croft is yours! Go to the factor in the morning—it was meant to be! Oh! that boy was born to be hanged—a proper rascal!' And she went on repeating this or something like it till I wondered Murdo did not tell her to shut up.

I listened intently, set on hearing what he answered. That was what mattered. Not Effie. I knew, I always had known that she was not to be trusted, that she would push us out if she could but what did he mean to do?

'The croft—' he muttered then. 'Aye! the croft, not one —not one but two crofts side by side and four cows and four calves.' (He was meaning the souming). He spoke dreamily like a man talking of some wonderful good fortune he did not hope to gain.

'Maggie's a grand worker! You and Maggie! You'd win a good harvest, plenty of food for the cows and oats for the mill—'

I could not see Effie. She must be sitting opposite Murdo, directly below me. I could not see Mother either but the corner she always sat in was out of sight.

'Maggie's laid by a wee bit, a tidy wee bit, enough to buy a cow or two! She's been a good daughter to me and she'll make you a good wife, Murdo.'

At that he turned and stared as if in wonder. But surely this was no surprise. Archie had said months ago that he was courting Maggie.

'Aye!—a croft—two crofts—a wife!' and he gave a kind of bark. I suppose it passed for a laugh with him. He said this three times over and clapped his knee and then I knew what was wrong. He was drunk. He must have been in all day with Effie and she'd been pouring raw whisky into him from a shebeen. That was why he talked so strangely as if marrying Maggie were quite a new and odd idea while when he was sober it was plain common sense. Effie's voice rose as if she were not all that pleased with the way things were going.

'You go to the factor yourself, Murdo,' she urged. 'Don't leave it to that gaumless Mackay. *You* tell him what's happening to the sheep, to your sheep, Murdo, and who's at the bottom of it all—'

'Aye!' he let out a bellow all of a sudden, 'that red-headed fellow. If I had him here I'd choke him!'

My heart was in my throat! I'd heard enough. Time to be off. I'd better be careful. I slowly inched my way along the back of the house meaning to put the dyke between me and harm. Perhaps if I'd run for it? But then things would have worked out differently. The thought of the dogs worried me. So long as I was motionless they did not come near me but as soon as I moved one came sniffing round. I still had the fish and I threw him another one. That would give me time. I meant to step gently to the dyke but my nerve broke and I ran. Round the end of the house came the other dog and behind him Murdo. I flung the last of the fish at the dog and leaped over the dyke. I had landed on soft ground and lost seconds dragging my feet clear.

'At him! At him! Marsco!'

The fish were no use, the dogs came for me. I beat off the first, snapping at my throat, but the second leaped and brought me down, the two of them breathing heavy above my head. Next moment Murdo had me in his grip and yanked me to my feet.

'Got you! Got you!' he exulted. 'I knew I would if I waited long enough.'

He dragged me into the house like a man dragging a sheep into a fank.

'Got him!' he shouted. Effie let out a kind of skirl.

'Oh Murdo, are you not the clever one! Where was he?'

'Behind the house, just making away but I got him!'

With two savage dogs it wasn't all that difficult, I thought. Next moment he had his face close to mine and the reek of his breath made my stomach heave.

'Where were you last night?'

'Aye! tell him that!' cried Effie. 'You tell him that!'

'I was out poaching,' I said as coolly as I could. I knew I was done for but still I'd try.

'Poaching! Poaching!' he repeated. He was so far gone in drink he kept saying the word as if he did not know the meaning.

'Poaching!' cried Effie. 'Oh! dear me, yes, horses!' She hadn't drunk so much or else she stood it better, her wits

were not all astray, 'and the sheep Murdo, that you'd been
all day gathering what did he do to your sheep?'

She was like Tomas playing with a mouse, almost purring
with pleasure as she set Murdo on to me—Effie and Murdo
with me between them in the fire-lit kitchen, full of shadows.

'The sheep!' Murdo's breath came fast and his iron grip
tightened. 'You let them out! Left that gate open and let
them out and me out all day from morn to night gathering
them and you let them out!'

With each repetition he shook me till my teeth chattered.
I was without hope now. Murdo minded about the sheep
like a man minding about his own children. It wasn't just
letting those out of the fank but the ones I was chasing up
Ben Lee every morning.

'You're at them the whole time, the whole time! And the
factor doesn't stop you but I'll stop you! You won't chase
Black Murdo's sheep any more!'

And with the last word he flung me with all his force
against the wall. I flung up my arm and my elbow came
crack against the stone. I let out a yell. The pain was so
bad that everything went black.

I don't know how long it was till I came to. Not long, I
guess for Murdo was still standing just where he'd been.
He'd finish the business this time I thought. He'd smash my
brains out. I heard loud rasping breathing and wondered who
was breathing like that and with a shock knew it was I
myself. But why was he silent? What was keeping him
from shouting at me?

I twisted my head and saw him but he was not looking
at me but at something in the corner. But what made him
look so strange, jaw dropping, and eyes staring? He backed
away and now I saw Mother move a step forward, one step,
no more. Her hands were clasped in front of her.

With one hand Murdo was feeling for the door latch
behind him. He did not turn but kept his eyes fixed on
Mother.

Effie must have seen her last chance slipping from her. 'Take no heed of her, Murdo!' she shrieked. 'She's a poor witless creature that doesn't know what to do till I tell her! See this!' and she came close to Mother and said, 'Sit down! Do as I say—sit down!'

My breath caught in my throat. Would she? And leave Murdo to finish me off? No, she ignored Effie completely but still she looked at Murdo, her hands clasped and took another step.

'No!' he gave a strangled shout. 'No! no, no, don't touch me, don't!' His fumbling fingers found the latch and threw it up. He pulled open the door and stumbled out.

There was a moment's silence, the three of us fixed in our place then Effie hirpled after him shouting, 'Murdo! Murdo! Come back, come back!'

I got to my feet, pulling myself up by my right arm. I swayed and staggered but I reached the door, went out and closed it behind me. The fresh air came sweet to my nostrils. I could still hear Effie's clamour. I waited. I waited.

In the field the corncrake called and called. I waited. Then I heard the shuffle, shuffle of her old feet, dragging. She was close to me now, muttering. She saw me, hesitated, stopped.

'Go away!' I said. 'Go away!' That was all, only these two words twice over but all my force behind them.

Effie peered at me, took a step forward, hesitated and then shuffled slowly out of sight.

I leaned back against the door trembling, weak as a new born lamb. She'd gone! I'd made her go! *Made* her! The wonder of it filled me. But Mother—

I went in, spoke her name. 'Mother! You saved my life.'

She was back again in her old corner plucking at the threads in her skirt. She never looked at me.

I smoored the fire. I thought of food but a wave of nausea came over me. I went through to my own bed. I could do no more.

18 'The Tide Is In'

The wonder is I woke at all but some bit of my brain must have stayed on guard for I found myself out on the floor listening. But listening for what? What had wakened me? Black Murdo? Was he back? Or was it Effie? I felt my hair rise and my legs tremble under me. I took a step to the door, opened it, listened again. Not a sound! I must have been dreaming. I'd go back to bed. I'd just see if Mother was all right first and then I could sleep easy. I crossed over to the kitchen, opened the door and could see plainly every corner with the blaze of the fire. I was amazed and then afraid. Effie must have come back! I jumped round fearing to find her behind me but the passage was empty. The bed too was empty, the curtain drawn aside.

Then it was Mother who had made up the fire and hung the big kettle on the chain! But she had done no work since the day of the fight! And where was she? Why had she gone out in the middle of the night?

I went to the door and there was Bess jumping up on me trying to lick my face.

'Bess! where have you been? Did you get out of the byre?' I had tied her up before I left to get the ponies. I petted her, I was so glad to see her. I felt the rope still round her neck. She had gnawed it through leaving a few feet dangling after her. It struck me then that she'd done the right thing for if Murdo had found her I'd have found her dead body. I gave her another pat—I was so pleased to have her with me and then I told her what had happened.

'We'll have to find Mother,' I said. It was a comfort to speak aloud after all those hours of being on my own.

Bess went into the lead exactly as if she were showing me the way. But could I trust her? She was only young and besides she hardly knew Mother. But as if to deny this I had a sudden picture of Mother's hand stroking Bess's head, why it was only a day or so ago. At that I made up my mind to follow her. She had her nose to the ground plainly scenting someone.

It wasn't dark exactly, not so dark as when we had crouched in the fank but there was a mist in the hollows. We went fast plunging down the bank of the burn and up the other side and then I heard the clink of a bucket striking a stone. Straining my eyes I could just see her. It looked as if she were making for her father's house and at that my heart lifted. She'd be safe there. She passed out of sight. The mist was thicker now, clinging to the hillside. Bess had caught up with Mother and was following at her heel.

When I got over the rise I could see Mother already away past grandfather's. I did not know what to think. There is no way of guessing what a sick person will do. I mean a person whose mind is sick. I must catch up with her and tell her to come back to grandfather's with me.

She was skirting the growing corn, quick and light on her feet, making me think of her as she used to be setting off for a day's work on the beach.

The path left the corn field and plunged down a hollow filled with wild rhubarb. It was there I caught up with her.

'Where are you going?' I cried and caught hold of her arm.

'Going!' she said surprised like and it was her own voice but as if she talked to a stranger. 'Going? To the beach to pick whelks. There's the rent to pay—and the little girls —they need—' And she was off again leaving me cold and shivery. The little girls had been dead these many years.

There was something I knew I should tell her, something which would stop her going down to the beach but I was stupid with fatigue. She was hurrying on, the thistles and goosegrass dragging at her skirt.

All of a sudden I remembered.

'Mother! Mother! The tide's in!'

But it was no use. She neither stopped nor answered but kept on. We reached the bay and she walked rapidly down the grass bank and down the rough, pebbly beach.

The high tide came almost to the grass and at once she was in the sea.

I ran shouting 'Mother! Can't you see? The tide's in, the tide's in. You can't pick whelks.'

She stood there, the water up to her knees.

'The tide!' was all she said, a look of astonishment on her face.

'Come back! Come back! You'll be wet through!'

But still she stood as if she could not understand the sea being where it was.

I was frightened. What if she went farther in? She could not swim and I was doubtful whether I could save her.

'Come back!' I said angrily. 'What do you think you're doing?'

I tugged at her arm and this time she let me help her back up the beach, her feet stumbling and the water squelching in her boots. She leaned heavily on my arm but once we had gained the grass bank she lay face down and wept.

I stood there in the dull light not knowing what to do. I was afraid to leave her alone and I was equally afraid I could not get her home without help. The mist had turned to rain and large drops pitted the smooth surface of the water. Bess sat patiently waiting and I knew I must wait too.

At long last she lifted her head, pushing the hair out of her eyes.

'Is it you, Sam?' I caught my breath. She knew me, she had used my name at last.

'Is it you, Sam?' she repeated. 'Where am I? Oh! Sam, I thought—I thought the little girls were alive and I was going to get money to buy things for them—the fishing's been bad.'

My heart contracted. 'They've been dead a long time!' The words burst out of me, loud and harsh.

'No, no, they were alive, they were with me—I hadn't lost them.'

'Don't talk like that! Don't! They're dead—dead! *I'm* alive.' We faced each other in the mist and the rain.

Then without another word she stretched out her hand and I pulled her up and we started on our road back. When we reached the narrow path she went ahead of me and I noticed how heavily she walked now and how passing once more through the wild rhubarb she trod down the stalks releasing their rank smell.

We reached grandfather's at last and there was great excitement and rejoicing. But I stood alone, tired and miserable.

I went to the door and heard the cocks crow, one near, one far. It was almost morning. But I wanted no morning, only sleep. I remembered Uncle Calum's empty bed. I shuffled out of my wet clothes, rolled myself in the blankets and was soon fast asleep.

When I woke grandfather was smiling down at me.

'I was just thinking of pouring a pail of water over you! Your grandmother is thinking the bed was damp and you're done for!'

Grandmother was always fussing about clothes being damp and so was Mother for that matter. Damp or not I'd slept soundly.

Now I was ravenously hungry and hurried into my clothes which had been dried for me.

In the kitchen the first thing I saw was Mother putting peats on the fire and when she saw me she smiled and I smiled back but I felt shy and did not know what to say.

Luckily with the grandparents both talking there was no

need for me to say anything and I could sit down to a plate
of cod and do it justice.

Well! that was one fish Murdo's dogs hadn't got. Grandmother was busy mixing a feed for the hens and that put
me in mind of my own. Good life! I hadn't fed them for
two days and Ian had left me in charge. I sprang up meaning
to be off there and then but grandfather told me to sit and
have a cup of tea at least. Seeing the hens had done without
for two days they'd not die for an hour or two yet. That was
true enough and as I was still hungry—after all I hadn't
eaten a bite since midday of the day before— I sat down.
Grandfather was in rare good humour teasing me about the
amount I ate and that I'd be hard to winter.

To excuse myself I said I had not eaten my share of the
fish, Murdo's dogs had got them.

'Murdo's dogs!' grandfather exclaimed. 'What are you
talking about, Sam?'

I stopped in the act of buttering my piece and looked
up. They were all staring at me. For a moment I was as
puzzled as they were. Didn't they know about Murdo's visit?
Hadn't Mother told them? And the next moment I saw how
stupid that was. Mother could not tell them what she did not
know herself though she was there.

So I told them all that had happened and my word, grandfather was in a state. I never saw him in such a taking and
he went straight out to his neighbour, Seumas to ask him
what he meant by telling us Murdo had gone.

He was back almost at once and Seumas with him.

'But I'm telling you, Alasdair, he passed me on the road in
Ollach and he was going at a fair pace. It was the truth I told
you! Why would I tell you anything else? I gave him a
good day but all he did was to nod.'

'He doubled back then! By the hill! I ought to have gone
with you last night, Sam! I might have guessed! I might have
known!' And then to Seumas, 'He might have killed the

lad and his brother away at sea and his mother—'

I'd never seen grandfather so upset. He'd been calmness itself meeting the sheriff officer, and even the policeman dragging him out of the house had not put him up or down.

Grandmother told him there was no use in worrying now. I had escaped so what was he making such a stir about? She examined my arm and found no bones broken. Indeed I scarcely felt it now though I had fainted with pain at the time.

I had to go over the whole story several times. Was it not wonderful, they said, an act of Providence that Mother had saved me without knowing what she was doing.

'Do you remember nothing at all, Mhairi?'

Mother put a hand to her head as if it ached.

'We shouldn't be troubling you!'

'No, no, it does not harm me. I remember feeling that someone was in danger. Yes, I think that was it but it is all cloudy—I think I heard a cry and I got up and I stood —but that is all—'

We were silent thinking what might have happened if she had not heard me.

'He was mad with rage!' I said. 'I'd chased his sheep.' I knew how he felt and just for a moment I was sorry for him but I would never feel sorry for Effie nor ever forget how she had gloated when Murdo had dragged me in. I shuddered though it was broad daylight and I was safe. But thinking of Effie put me in mind of the cows. But even then grandfather would not let me go.

'I'll get someone to milk,' he told me, 'you stay here and have a rest. You've done enough.'

Well! I wasn't at all sorry to do just that.

When grandfather came back we asked him who went to milk.

'Chrissie,' he said cheerfully, 'she's a bright lass and a good worker.'

Chrissie! Having to milk my cows! I'd never hear the

end of it! Her tongue was bad enough when I wasn't asking favours at all. Grandfather told me they'd all been asking for me. The news flashed from house to house, the news of my escape and Mother's recovery.

It was late that night when grandmother said something which made things clearer to me. Mother had gone to bed for she tired easily, and I was yawning and saying I'd go too and make up for lost sleep.

Grandfather gave a snort. 'Lost sleep indeed! and you snoozing under the blankets at noon!'

'You just think what the boy went through!' said grandmother sharply and then I expect she wished she hadn't for it set grandfather off once more wishing he'd gone with me.'

'I'll never forgive myself, Mor. What would Ian have said to me when he came home if anything had happened to Sam?'

But grandmother shook her head.

'You're not seeing this right, Alasdair, you're not understanding how Providence worked. If you had gone up with Sam and dealt with Black Murdo and the boy had never been in danger Mhairi might not have come back! It was the shock that brought her back—as far as the little girls and then the high tide and Sam himself brought her the rest of the way and we should be thankful.'

Grandfather sat in silence for a wee while taking this in and then he nodded.

'You're right, Mor. You have the truth of it, I do believe.'

At that I went off to bed with a light heart.

19 *Ben Lee*

On midsummer's day we put the sheep up Ben Lee. There was a great crying of lambs and bleating of ewes as we drove them slowly upwards. The dew was heavy on the grass and on the spiders' webs, stretched between clumps of heather. Mist lay like a fleece over the summit. Behind us the sun fought clear of the clouds and at once our long shadows pointed the way ahead. Larks were singing and a hare started up from our feet and fled in zigzags up the slope. We kept the dogs from giving chase for they had their business to see to. Bess kept close to my heel, eyes bright, ears pricked for the least sound. I was as proud as a prince. I'd make a good dog of her now.

The men stopped, whistling to us boys to turn back. 'Are we just going home?' asked Donald, a world of disappointment in his voice.

'Won't there be a fight?' said another. 'Och! this is no use.'

The men overheard them. Neil was leaning on his crook and gazing at the top from which the cloud was slowly clearing.

'We're not at the end yet, lads, take it from me! Dear knows what the landlord may do. They say he's sending a factor from the east coast to value the crofts. He'll put a high value on them, I wouldn't wonder!'

The men stood there arguing, weighing up the different moves that might be made by Alasdair Ruadh (the old fox wasn't beaten yet!), by the mysterious commission and Parliament itself.

The boys ran off and I followed. I had a feeling, I don't know why, but it was strong in me, that we had won. I had not expected that morning any stand up fight with

Black Murdo. The last time I had seen him he was a beaten man.

I halted and looked back. The crying of the lambs was dying out as each one found its mother. The flock was scattering peacefully over the pasture. So it amounted to this. We had taken the hill back and no one, not factor or tenant or shepherd, would take it from us any more. And all at once I was back in Kemp's room in Portree and Charles Ramsay was leaning on the mantelpiece and smiling down at me. 'You'll get your hill back yet, Sam!' he had said and we had! we had!

There was just the one person I had not seen since mother's recovery. I often thought of her. Was she still angry with me, I wondered, but I hadn't the courage to go and find out.

Then she came to see us; I was indoors that morning for the rain was drumming down outside. Every now and then a drop came through and sizzled on the hot girdle. Mother was busy baking and I was whittling away at a hazel root meaning to make a shepherd's crook out of it but it would take time.

All at once Bess growled, the door opened and there she was, a plaid over her head and the raindrops in her hair. Mother welcomed her, took her plaid, placing it over a chair to dry. 'I've come to say how glad we are—Mother and I—that you are well again, a Mhairi Alasdair,' said Jean in that soft voice I remembered so well. Mother thanked her, asked after *her* mother and there the talk languished. Mother unhooked the girdle from its chain above the fire and slung the kettle in its place. 'And how are you, Sam?' Jean asked, turning to look at me, 'we haven't seen a sight of you this while back.'

Was it likely I would go near their house seeing the scolding she had given me that day? I blushed to the roots of my hair and hadn't a word to say but Mother came to my rescue. 'He's that busy! They made him shepherd for the township and my word! if the ewes don't do well, it won't be Sam's fault for he's out after them early and late. It's just the morning being so wet that's kept him in today.'

'I'm sure he's a good shepherd!' Jean replied and then she spoke of her father and the *Seagull*. He was hoping to be home in a month or so. Mother nodded. Yes! she had had a letter from Ian telling her the fishing was good. She busied herself making tea and when it had brewed, poured Jean a cup and gave her a piece of bannock. They chatted of this and that but I felt a kind of constraint too as if they were not sure of each other and this surprised me for I'd never seen Mother anything but open and friendly before.

At length Jean rose to go. Mother handed her the plaid and she put it over her head, her dark hair peeping out and framing her pretty face. 'Come a piece of the road with me, Sam,' she said, standing in the doorway. I believe I'd have cut and run if there had been another door but since there wasn't I got reluctantly to my feet and followed her.

We had to walk in single file along the path at the edge of the corn till we reached the far side of it and there she stopped to let me come beside her.

'We were missing you, Sam. I was wishing you'd come to see me.' I did not know what to say nor where to look so she hurried on. 'I was that sorry I had spoken so rough to you.' But here I lifted my head and stared at her in surprise. 'You only said what was true!' I blurted out. She smiled and blushed looking prettier than ever. 'Oh, no, Sam, what I said wasn't true. It was just, just, oh! I was in a temper —you'd made me angry and—'

But I did not let her go on. 'Jean! you know very well I was in the wrong—misdoubting Ian—and you—you—were quite right to say what you did.'

But Jean shook her head. 'No, no, Sam, I was ashamed of myself. You were having a hard time and I made it worse.' I considered this. 'Aye! I was burdened indeed but that did not excuse me believing Effie. Oh! good grief. I've known Effie all my life and she's always busy miscalling somebody. I didn't need to be such a cod's head taking her lies for gospel.' I shivered recollecting that dreadful time and glanced behind me as if expecting to see her shuffling to our door but there was no one. Only the smoke from her chimney told me she was still there.

'I understand, Sam, I guessed how it was afterwards and I was longing to see you to put matters right but there was no sign of you and after that I was hearing you were a hero! I thought maybe you'd chase such low company as me away!' We both laughed out loud while the rain poured down and we never noticed it.

'When will you be married?' I asked as bold now as I'd been backward before.

'What!' she exclaimed, 'are you asking for me?'

'I would and all if I'd had the luck to be born ahead of *him*.'

'My word, Sam, you'll be a one for the girls in a year or two! Well, if you want to know, we're hoping to be married in the autumn when the harvest's in.'

'Will you have a "banais"?'

'What do you think! We'll be killing cockerels and plucking hens for a week beforehand!'

What a feast that would be and what fun we would have.

'And then you'll be my sister and live up on the moor!'

She made a little face at me and then smiled. 'Run home, Sam, or you'll be wet through' and she picked up her skirt and ran as light as a fawn down the path.

'Well, just look at you,' grumbled Mother. 'Soaking wet! What did the lassie have to say that you took such a time?'

'Oh, nothing, nothing.' I was pleased to have a secret of my own. 'She was just passing the time of day.'

'She could choose a drier one!' remarked Mother.

I grinned to myself and fondled Bess's ears. She had crawled back in under the settle with just her head showing. 'A banais!' I said to myself—what a feast that would be, and to Bess I whispered, 'I'll keep the bones for you.'